"Orca Tales is a compelling and heartrending journey into the world of Orcas, a must-read that beautifully intertwines a captivating narrative with a powerful message of wildlife conservation."

"Orca Tales is a riveting, eye-opening testament to the urgent need for wildlife conservation."

—Reprospace Reviews™

Orca Tales

Charles P. Howerton

Published by Kitsap Publishing
Poulsbo, WA 98370
www.KitsapPublishing.com

Acknowledgments

To Helen E. Erickson, My Friend, My Muse, My Love.

Writing "An Orca's Tale" has been a journey of discovery, passion, and dedication. This book would not have been possible without the support, guidance, and encouragement of many individuals and organizations.

First and foremost, I would like to express my deepest gratitude to the *Metropolitan State College of Denver*, where I spent many rewarding years as a Computer Science Professor. The university's *Department of Earth and Atmospheric Sciences* commitment to fostering curiosity and promoting research has been an inspiration in my journey.

I am profoundly grateful to the various marine conservation organizations worldwide for their tireless efforts to protect our oceans and their inhabitants. Your work has been a constant source of inspiration and has provided invaluable insights for this book.

Special thanks to my colleagues in the academic and scientific community. Your rigorous discussions and insightful feedback have greatly enriched this work.

I would also like to acknowledge the countless marine biologists and researchers whose work forms the backbone of this narrative. Your dedication to understanding and preserving marine life is truly commendable.

To my family and friends, thank you for your unwavering support and patience throughout the writing process. Your belief in the importance of this story has been a driving force behind its completion.

Finally, I would like to dedicate this book to the Orcas, the majestic creatures who are the heart of this tale. It is my hope that this book will contribute to a greater understanding and appreciation of these remarkable beings and the urgent need for their conservation.

Thank you all for being a part of this journey.

Charles P. Howerton

Foreword

by the Publisher

As the publisher of "*Orca Tales*," it is with great pride and a sense of responsibility that we bring this important work to you. This book is not just a story; it is a testament to the enduring spirit of wildlife and the relentless dedication of those who work tirelessly to protect it.

In the pages that follow, you will be introduced to a world that is both awe-inspiring and heart-wrenching. The narrative is set against the backdrop of the majestic Pacific Northwest, home to the magnificent Orca, also known as the killer whale. The story that unfolds is one of courage, compassion, and an urgent call to action.

The author masterfully weaves together the threads of human and animal lives, creating a tapestry that is as rich in emotion as it is in its message. The characters you will meet are not just characters in a book, but embodiments of the real heroes who stand on the front lines of wildlife conservation.

"Orca Tales" is more than a book; it is a movement. It is a plea for understanding, a call for respect, and a rallying cry for all of us to take a stand. It is our hope that as you turn each page, you will not only be moved by the story but also be inspired to become a part of the solution.

As a publisher, we believe in the power of words to change hearts and minds. But words alone are not enough. It is action that brings about change. And so, we invite you to not just read this book, but to let it move you to action.

Together, we can make a difference. Together, we can ensure that the tale of the Orca is not just a tale of struggle, but ultimately, a tale of survival.

Thank you for joining us on this journey.

Ingemar Anderson, Kitsap Publishing

Introduction

Welcome to "Orca Tales," a narrative that takes you on a journey into the depths of the Pacific Northwest and into the lives of its most iconic inhabitants, the Orcas or killer whales. This book is more than a story; it is a reflection of our relationship with the natural world and a call to action for its preservation.

In the chapters that follow, you will witness the profound impact of human actions on these magnificent creatures. You will be introduced to a cast of characters who, in the face of adversity, dedicate their lives to the rescue and treatment of an injured Orca. Their stories are a testament to the power of compassion, collaboration, and unwavering dedication.

However, "Orca Tales" is not just about the struggle for survival; it is also about hope. It is about the potential for change when we choose to respect and protect the wildlife with whom we share our world. It is about the difference each one of us can make when we choose to act.

As you delve into this book, we invite you to not just read, but to reflect, to question, and to act. Consider the role each of us plays in the preservation or destruction of our natural world. Ask yourself what you can do to make a difference.

"Orca Tales" is a mirror held up to our society, reflecting both our failures and our potential for change. It is our hope that as you turn the last page, you will be moved to become a part of the solution, to contribute to a future where the tale of the Orca is one of survival, not struggle.

Thank you for embarking on this journey with us. Let the tale begin.

Understanding Orca Communications

In this book, you will notice the use of brackets [ ] instead of traditional quotation marks to indicate communication with and between Orcas. This stylistic choice is intended to emphasize the unique nature of these interactions, which are unlike human conversation and often involve a combination of sounds, gestures, and other non-verbal cues. For example, a dialog with an Orca will look like this:

"Okay," she said as she reached out to touch the animal again. [Not so strongly] I heard Jill telepathically tell the big Orca.

[Why hurt we?] The Orca replied with less force.

Orcas, or killer whales, are known for their complex and sophisticated communication methods. They use a variety of vocalizations, including clicks, whistles, and calls, each with different frequencies and patterns. These sounds are used for navigation, hunting, and social interaction. Orcas also communicate through physical behaviors such as breaching, slapping the water with their tails or pectoral fins, and even through touch. Each pod of Orcas has its own unique dialect, a testament to their social structure and intelligence.

As you read, we invite you to imagine these extraordinary forms of communication and to appreciate the remarkable world of the Orcas.

Part I

Sonny's Tale

The Incident

Jenny Fuller was fixing lunch in the kitchen when the phone rang. Bob, her husband, picked up the receiver and, noting the caller ID, said, "Hi, Philomena, Jenny's in the kitchen. She'll be with you in a moment."

"Hi, Bob. Just tell her that Orcas are heading your way. I'm sure she'll want to know so she can watch them. No time to waste; I'm going out back right now to watch 'em myself before they go around the point." Philomena Carlson replied.

"Okay, Phil, I'll tell her. But, hey, why don't you come on over and watch with Jenny from here?" Bob said.

"Thanks, I'll do just that. I'll be there in five minutes."

"Take care, bye," Bob replied.

"Who was it, Bob?" Jenny asked.

"It was Phil, Hon. She said Orcas are heading our way, and you should go out back to watch for them. I invited her over to watch them with you. You go ahead; lunch can wait."

"Thanks, Love," Jenny said as she picked up her video camera case and rushed out the back door.

The Fullers had built an observation platform that extended out over the bluff at the north edge of their property. From it, Jenny had a perfect view of the Strait of Juan de Fuca from the point to the west near the Carson's house and east, almost to Discovery Bay.

When Philomena arrived, she went straight to the observation platform to join Jenny, who was getting her video camera mounted and ready. "Hi, Jenny. How can I help?" She asked.

"Hi, Phil. Would you please hand me the telephoto lens, the medium-sized one? It has a broader field of view." Jenny said.

"This one?"

"Yeah, that's the one," Jenny said as she took the lens and attached it to the camera body. She checked to be sure that everything was connected properly and turned on the camera and the video recorder.

"Okay, let's watch," she said, pulling up one of the two bar stools on the platform while her friend brought the other one over. They perched themselves at the railing on either side of the camera and watched the Orcas.

A few minutes later, Bob came out. "Hey ladies, I thought you might like to have some lunch." He said as he placed a tray loaded with sodas and sandwiches on the table. "Seen anything yet?"

"Oh, yeah. They're right over there," Jenny said, pointing toward the pod of Orcas.

Bob glanced at where Jenny was pointing. "Fantastic!" he said, "That's almost as close as they've ever been, isn't it? Enjoy yourselves. If you will excuse me, I have a baseball game that needs watching. Let me know if you need anything else."

Jenny and Phil shared a pair of binoculars as they watched the Orcas rising and diving. After a bit, they could hear a boat approaching rapidly from the west. Jenny looked for it out in the Strait and when she could not find it,. She leaned out over the railing and saw it just below, close to the shore. She watched as it got closer, expecting it to turn out into the Strait to avoid the Orcas.

"Here, Phil, you take the binoculars and keep an eye on the boat," Jenny said, handing the binoculars to her friend. "I'll keep the camera on the Orcas."

"Whoever's in that boat is either trying to scare the Orcas or hit them," Philomena said. "What can we do?"

"Not much from here except to record what happens." Jenny said, then added, as the boat seemed to aim right for the center of the pod, "I think they're really trying to hit the Orcas."

They watched quietly for a moment, then Phil exclaimed, "Oh, thank God, the Orcas are diving to get out of the way!" Then she screamed, "No, oh no! A young one just came up for air, and the boat drove right over it and hit it so hard the boat bounced."

"I got it on video, but I couldn't see the name of the boat, could you?"

"Nope, all I saw was the first letter of the name. it was an 'S,' I think. It was a blue and white boat with two people in it. The driver was wearing a blue cap, and the other one had on a yellow cap."

Both women were in tears when Bob ran out of the house to see what the fuss was about. He immediately took his wife into his arms to calm her and then added Phil to the hug as well.

"What happened?" He asked.

"Those SOBs," Philomena said through her sobs, pointing to the rapidly disappearing boat, "ran over a young Orca deliberately."

"Are you sure it was deliberate?" he asked.

"Absolutely," Jenny said. "They aimed right at the pod. The larger Orcas all dove to avoid the boat. But a smaller one had just come up for a breath when they aimed right at it and hit it. They did it deliberately, Bob. We watched it."

"Did you get it on your videotape?" He asked.

"I sure did. I had the camera pointed right at the pod when we heard the boat coming, and I kept it in view until after the boat hit the Orca and went roaring off."

"I saw the driver do an arm pump as they drove away," Philomena added.

"Did you see the Orcas after the boat passed? What did they do?" Bob asked.

"The larger ones surrounded the smaller ones, and they swam very slowly to the North, out into the Strait over towards the San Juan Islands," Jenny replied.

"Okay, we'll need to call and tell somebody. The Coast Guard, maybe, or NOAA or the game wardens, but it's a Saturday, so we might have to wait until Monday. Meanwhile, why don't you both go into the house, have a drink, and write down what you saw? I'm pretty sure it would be better if you did not collaborate in the writing. Two independent descriptions will be better than one. Eyewitness accounts are generally not considered to be very reliable. However, eyewitness accounts supported by a videotape will be golden." Bob said. "I'll bring in the camera and recorder and the rest of your stuff."

"Okay." Both ladies answered, still sniffing but more calmly.

"Thanks, Bob," Jenny said.

"Yes, thanks a lot," her friend seconded.

A Cry For Help

We were sitting in the semi-recliners in the back of our boat, basking in the sun and trolling as slowly as possible, fishing for the last salmon of our four-fish limit. There were already three five-pound silvers in the cooler, so it had been a successful day, but we still had some time before we had to start for home. The boat was steering itself, and at this speed, we were not likely to run into anything except maybe a piece of driftwood. We were actually dozing as we fished. Then, suddenly we felt a solid bump that came as a complete surprise. I knew we hadn't hit anything because the bump was not on the bow; it was on the left side of the boat, right behind where I was sitting. I was sure it wasn't another boat because I checked frequently to ensure there were no other boats nearby. So, it had to be that something had either washed into the side of the boat and hit us, or the bump was deliberate.

Jill, my wife, looked around and shouted, "Good grief, Jack, we are surrounded by Orcas."

I turned to look and saw the dorsal fin of an Orca, a killer whale. We often see Orcas when we are fishing and have had them steal our fish right off our lines, but we never had one come closer than 15 to 20 yards. Orcas generally steer clear of boats that are moving except to steal fish. They also usually avoid boats that are at anchor and aren't likely to be bumping into a boat under any circumstances. I immediately assumed if we hadn't hit anything, then something had hit us. Perhaps the carcass of a dead Orca had drifted into the boat. But this Orca was alive, giving out a series of high-pitched squeals, clicks, and whistles, then it bumped our boat again.

Jill took one look and immediately began to reel in her line, saying, "Jack do you think we have snagged an Orca with our trolling lures?"

"I hope not," I replied as I also began to reel in my line. The last thing we needed in an older twenty-foot plywood cabin cruiser was to be rammed by six tons or more of pissed-off Orca playing Moby Dick. Then I thought, even if it had been hooked, why would it be banging on the side of our boat? It could have just taken off, dragging out the line until it either ran out or broke or the hook pulled free. All of this ran through my mind in an instant. I looked at Jill, shrugged, and stood up. I signaled her to stay put and then went over to see what was happening.

Jill reacted with, "Good grief, Jack, be careful!"

I looked over the side and into the eye of an animal almost as long as our boat and a lot bigger, an animal that is reputed to be dangerous, but I did not get the feeling of being threatened. On the contrary, it seemed to me that it was trying to get our attention. It squealed, whistled, and clicked again and then raised its head above the water, sky-scoping as Orcas often do when they want to see what is on the surface around them. Then, without stopping to think, I reached out and touched the side of the Orca's head.

"Jack, no!" Jill shouted as I touched the animal.

[WE HURT!] It came blasting into my head so powerfully that it stunned me for a moment.

As a reflex, I replied, [Not so loud.] Without realizing it, I replied both vocally and mentally. Jill heard me, and I heard her startled gasp, then felt her hand on my shoulder.

Immediately, the reply, [We hurt], came at a more moderate intensity level. I 'heard' it just as clearly as I might hear someone speaking to me. At the same time, the mental image of a smaller Orca swimming beside a large Orca came into my mind. I could see that the smaller Orca was in distress.

Jill heard and saw it through me, "Oh my God!" she exclaimed.

[Where?] I asked at an equally moderate level, again both aloud and mentally, which is what I would do from then on.

[Come], was the reply a request or an order? I continued touching the Orca during the exchange, and I felt the connection break as it began to swim away.

Jill had finished reeling in the trolling lines and killed the trolling motor.

"Did you get that?" I asked.

"Some of it." She replied.

"What did you get?"

"I got an image of a young Orca and a feeling of intense pain." Jill has always been more empathetic than me.

"Jeez, that was amazing; I 'heard' that as clearly as when we do telepathy," I said.

"What are we going to do?"

"Follow along and see what is going on, I guess."

"Okay, Captain." She said, throwing me a mock salute. "Fire it up, and let's go."

While we were stowing our fishing gear and preparing to follow, the Orca returned and bumped the boat again while squealing and clicking. By this time, I realized that the Orca was a female because she had a shorter and more erect dorsal fin as opposed to the taller and often drooping fin of the male.

I reached out and touched her again and heard, [Come!] This time there was a definite sense of urgency in the message, almost a plea.

[We are coming.] I thought back at her and started the engine. As she swam away, we followed.

We were near the San Juan Islands in the Strait of Juan de Fuca on the American side of the line between Washington State and Vancouver Island, British Columbia. There are several pods and family groups of Orcas in the San Juan islands that are closely tracked and monitored by various officials and volunteer groups. Killer whale watching cruises are a summer tourist industry. There are often twenty or more boats in the area tracking the whales so tourists can see them and take pictures. Strict rules govern how close the boats are allowed to go to the Orcas. It was late afternoon when the Orca bumped us. The whale-watching boats had all returned to their home ports, and there were no other boats in sight; we were alone with the Orcas.

The Orcas swam towards one of the smaller, uninhabited islands. We followed at what I estimated was the legal 200-yard distance as mandated by the Washington State Department of Fish and Wildlife (WDFW) and a couple of federal agencies.

I received occasional fragments of an image or a word when the Orca squealed and clicked, but nothing like what I 'saw and heard' when I touched her. Nevertheless, we had established rapport, and I knew it would get better as we adapted to each other. I also understood that only some things the Orca sent were intended for me because sometimes I received nothing when she made her sounds.

She led us around to the western side of the island and into a small cove with a sandy beach. There we found a small pod of about ten animals, including what I assumed to be the younger one whose image the Orca had shown me. The younger Orca was evident from its shorter and smaller dorsal fin.

I cut the engine, and Jill went forward to drop the anchor. I was careful to maintain the allowable distance from the pod as I had no desire to be ticketed by the WDFW or the Coast Guard. The boat drifted for a few seconds on its forward momentum until the anchor took hold. As soon as we stopped, we were surrounded by what looked like the entire pod except for the young one, and all of them were making Orca sounds furiously. Several of the Orcas came up and touched the boat gently or as gently as an excited six-ton whale's touch could be.

Jill reached out to touch one, and I heard her gasp and stagger back.

"Too strong?" I asked.

"Yeah, and it's really pissed!"

"At us?"

"I don't know."

"Ask it, but first tell it to not send so loudly."

"Okay," she said as she reached out to touch the animal again. [Not so strongly] I heard Jill telepathically tell the big Orca.

[Why hurt we?] The Orca replied with less force.

[Who hurt you?] Jill asked.

[Boat hurt we!]

[How?]

The Orca projected an image of a blue and white speed boat tearing across the water and hitting the younger Orca just as it rose to breathe. We both got the image. No words were needed.

[When?] Jill asked.

The reply was a jumble of confusing images that meant nothing to either of us right away. When we sorted it out, what we saw was the image of a boat hitting the youngster from the point of view of many members of the pod. Some images were highly distorted views of the incident, which we realized were echolocation as the

Orca saw it. Unfortunately, none of the images gave us any indication of when the boat had hit the young Orca. The images of the boat itself did not give us enough information to identify which boat it was or who was driving.

"Ask it to have the young one come over here by the boat." I said.

Jill reached over and, touching the nearest Orca, sent the request.

The reply was very intense but modulated so as not to overpower us. [We fear.]

[Then why did you come to us?] Jill asked. That is not exactly what she asked but a transliteration. The human brain is a marvelous organ that fills in gaps automatically in sight, sound, and apparently telepathy. We found as we were learning to read each other years ago that saying the message aloud at the same time as you think to send it telepathically helps initially to establish rapport.

[We heard you.] Next came a series of clicks and squeals and an image of a female that we assumed was the one who came for us, followed by, [Wanted help.] I was now receiving again even though I was not touching the Orca. My brain was rapidly adapting to the Orca's language and was starting to fill in appropriate syntax to improve understanding, including, I supposed, additional information the Orca was sending. The image of the Orca who came after us was intensely feminine and suggestive of motherhood, so my brain substituted 'Mother', and the cleaned-up and the adapted message came out as [We heard you. Mother wanted your help.]

[You heard us?] Jill asked in amazement.

[Yes, when you talked to each other, we could hear you. We thought you might be like us, but you are humans.]

I answered that [We are humans. But, we are like you in some ways.] I had to repeat that twice while the Orca's brain tried to reduce the message to Orca syntax, we didn't know enough of their language to say it perfectly, but they got the essence of the message.

[Not like us! Hurt us!] Jill was right. This one was pissed.

[We did not hurt you. We came when Mother asked us.] Jill sent.

About this time, "Mother" came back over to the boat. [Can you help us?] She asked in what seemed like a more friendly tone.

[Maybe,] I replied. [I must touch the young one.]

[Young one fears boat.]

[I will get in the water.] I sent it back. Then I went down into the cabin to get one of the wet suits I keep on the boat in case I need to go into the water to fix something. The water temperature in the Strait is typically 51 degrees Fahrenheit. Thermal shock can set in within minutes without a wet suit.

As an afterthought, I asked, [You will not hurt me?]

[We will not hurt you] Was the immediate reply.

I did the wetsuit backward, plop over the side into the frigid water. My body acclimated quickly, and I was ready to swim. To my surprise, the water was not as cold as I expected it to be. Then I realized that we were on the island's western side in shallow water, and it was late afternoon on a sunny summer day. The water was still fairly cool, but kids at beaches in the area regularly swim in water that is between 60 and 70 degrees, and my guess was the water was in the mid-sixties.

[Come.] Mother directed.

I started swimming after her but was quickly left behind. [Wait,] I sent.

[Hurry!]

[I cannot go any faster.] I replied.

Mother emitted a series of clicks and whistles, and moments later, I felt a surge at my feet, and I was being pushed from behind. I slid up the nose and along the back of the Orca that was pushing me. When I reached the dorsal fin, I held on, and in less than a minute, I was near the injured Orca. The ride was a fantastic surprise.

I slid off the back of the Orca I thought of as 'Pusher' and swam over to the young Orca. I intentionally swam around to the head to make sure it could see me. I reached out my hands and touched the animal to try to communicate with it. What came back was [Hurt. Fear] is more emotional than verbal. The message was messy because the young one was terrified, and feelings of anxiety and dread were unquestionably there.

[I will not hurt you.] I sent.

Again came [Pain. Fear.] as the young Orca quivered.

Mother came up to the young one and, with a very long and complex series of squeals and clicks, which made no sense to me, calmed the young Orca to the point where it was just quivering slowly in ripples from head to tail.

I swam back along the side of the animal to the place where I could see several cuts, most likely from the keel or propeller of the boat that hit it. I have seen similar cuts on seals, dolphins, porpoises, and other sea animals over the years, mostly in the form of scars. I was puzzled at the level of pain this animal was broadcasting as a skin cut though blubber was not usually very severe. Then, I noticed a deeper gouge and missing skin across the back between the tail and the dorsal fin. I reached to touch it, and the animal flinched. When a three-ton animal flinches, the energy is intense. A side-swipe of the tail pushed me away, and, at the same time, I sensed the severe pain the animal was feeling as it pushed me.

Mother immediately gave another lengthy message to the young one to calm him down. Then she touched me with her head, apparently to keep it private, and sent, [Can you help?]

[Yes, I think so.] I replied.

Jill and I were both Army Medics in the Middle East War, where we met. We learned from medics in an allied service that they had received training in using an energy-healing technique called Healing Hands to calm and sometimes even heal injured soldiers.

Since then, we have had training in several other energy healing modalities and have become masters in several different forms of the art. In addition, we have used Healing Hands to treat each other, our friends, family, neighbors, and pets for years.

This was not the first time we had really communicated with animals. We were often able to 'hear' our dogs and cats, but they did not communicate in words, concepts, or images. We mostly just got feelings of one sort or another, like love or hunger, and we would try to send messages such as "Go lie down" or "Do you want to go out" with mixed results.

Orcas are apparently extremely organized and very intelligent. So I figured trying energy healing on the young Orca probably wouldn't hurt. However, to do that, I needed to touch the animal or be very close to it, and it clearly wasn't happy at being touched.

[Mother, I can help. I must touch him.] I said as I touched the young Orca. I sent this to Mother so he could hear it as well. How I knew the baby was a "him" was something I must have picked up from Mother without being aware of it.

"What are you doing?" Jill shouted across the water; it was too far for us to communicate telepathically.

"I'm going to try to give him a Healing Hands treatment." As I said this, I looked toward her and saw that she was already putting on her wet suit.

"I thought so; wait for me."

"Okay."

While Jill and I were talking, Mother was communicating with the young Orca, who was replying quietly.

[He is ready.] Mother said to me. It was a little jumbled because it was covered with concern.

Jill jumped into the water and started towards us. Mother immediately directed one of the other Orcas to tow her over to us.

"Wow, that was quite a ride," Jill said as she arrived. "It was sending something like, '[It will not hurt.]' It was trying to send calming thoughts to me. Can you believe that?"

"After the past half hour, I can believe anything," I replied.

"I'll get on the other side," Jill said. "Tell Mother to tell him that I will be there, please."

"You can tell her. She is very receptive now."

Before I could do anything, Mother sent, [He will be calm. Please help him.]

Jill had been sending it without being consciously aware of it. That's how I found out Jill was telepathic; then I let her know that I could 'hear' her. After that, she could 'hear' me as well.

[Okay, Mother, tell him to relax. We will not hurt him. We will just touch him and send him healing.] Heaven only knows what she received of that as I tried to reassure her of our good intentions. At the same time, I was very nervous about what might happen once we began. Energy healing is not always immediately soothing. Sometimes there is some discomfort as the body absorbs the energy and directs it to where it is needed for healing, but that usually goes away fairly quickly.

Mother once again 'spoke' to the young one. I overheard parts of what she sent, and the young one's identity felt like 'Sonny' to me.

The instant I touched Sonny in the area where he'd seemed to be the most sensitive, I felt him quiver all over. When Jill touched him, the quivering stopped, and I felt him relax. I think, if he could have, he would have sighed. Jill has a great touch.

We both began to channel healing energy into the area where he seemed to hurt the most. It quickly became apparent that Sonny had a severely sprained back in addition to the gouge where the boat had hit him. Most of his cuts were trivial compared to the deepest cut, which was certainly not trivial by any means. But, neither was it life-threatening. As for the area of the gouge, as anyone who has experienced a sprained back will tell you, there are few things more painful than a sprained back. In this case, the sprain was between his dorsal fin and tail. Every movement of his flukes was agony for him.

Mother made some comments to Sonny, and he replied quietly. Then he slowly began to move his flukes up and down as wave after wave of the healing energy flowed into his body. Finally, we could feel him relax from the tension that often accompanies back injuries as he began to lose the feeling of pain.

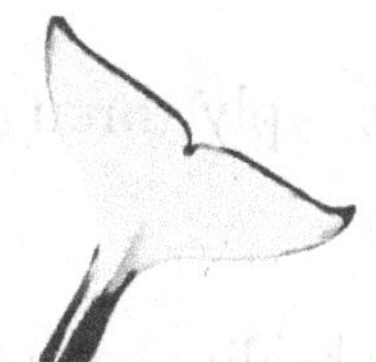

Coast Guard to the Rescue

We had been working on Sonny for over an hour when we heard a large boat come to the mouth of the cove and throttle down. Then we heard, "This is the U. S. Coast Guard. You are in violation of whale contact regulations. Come away from the whales and get out of the water immediately." Officialdom spoke through a bullhorn.

Within seconds, the Orcas surrounded the Coast Guard cutter, and several placed themselves between the ship and us. I have no idea whether or not the whales understood the order, but they made it plain that we were not to be bothered.

I shouted to the Cutter, "We're almost finished; we will be there in a few minutes."

The bullhorn clicked on as if the speaker was going to say something else and then clicked off again. Only the calling of the seagulls interrupted the silence for twenty more minutes. I could see the Cutter now and realized they were getting ready to lower a boat.

"We're nearly finished. We'll come to you." I shouted.

"Roger, that!" came the reply through the bullhorn at a much lower volume.

When one gives energy healing, one can sense when the session is over by the feeling in the hands. In my case, they would gradually stop tingling as the client's ability to absorb the energy diminishes. Jill sensed it differently as a sort of 'knowing' that she finished. When we doubled up, we almost always felt finished simultaneously.

[Better?] I asked Sonny.

[Better!] Was the emphatic reply followed by very strong feelings of contentment or gratitude?

[Mother, we are finished for now, and we must leave.] I sent.

Mother, too, sent feelings of gratitude, and a second or two later, we could feel the same feelings from the entire pod.

[Mother, we will be back tomorrow to see how he is.]

[We will wait.] she replied.

We started to swim back to our boat and had not gone more than a few yards before each of us had an Orca giving us a ride.

"Come here." The bullhorn squawked, followed by a quieter "Please."

I sent an image of going to the Cutter to my pusher, and it turned toward the Cutter. Jill and her pusher did the same. When we arrived at the Cutter, ladders were lowered over the side so we could climb aboard. On deck, we faced a surprised and puzzled Coast Guard crew who didn't know whether to be angry, astounded or confused.

"Welcome aboard," a four-striper said pleasantly as he extended his hand. "I'm Captain Elliot Miller, Commander of the Coast Guard station in Port Angeles."

"Pleased to meet you, Captain, I'm Jack Kline, and this is my wife Dolores, but please call her Jill everyone else does," I replied, returning the handshake. Captain Miller was taller than my 5 foot 10 inches and obviously fit. He had ice blue eyes and salt and pepper hair, more salt than pepper, under his USCG baseball cap.

"I'm not usually aboard the cutter," Captain Miller explained. "We were on our way back from a training seminar in Tacoma. Lieutenant Juanita Hernandez," he said, indicating a petite attractive woman standing beside him, "She is the actual Skipper of the cutter."

Lieutenant Hernandez offered her hand, "Pleased to meet you, Mr. and Mrs. Kline." She said with a pleasant smile. Her darker coloring and short, jet-black ponytail which was pulled back through the hole in the back of her baseball cap, bespoke Hispanic ancestry.

"And we are delighted to meet you both," Jill said as she returned Lt. Hernandez's handshake. "You don't sound southwestern," she continued.

"I get that a lot." Lt. Hernandez laughed, "I'm actually from Cleveland, but my grandparents were from New Mexico.

While this was going on, I turned back to Captain Miller, who clearly had some questions bothering him.

"Just what were you doing over there with the whales?" he asked, and before I could answer, "Don't you know it is against the law to get that close to them?"

"We know, Captain. They came to us for help. One of the pods, a juvenile, was hit by a boat and is seriously injured. They needed help."

The Captain stood looking first at us and then toward the Orcas while trying to think of what to say in reply. His mouth moved as if to speak, but he said nothing. Instead, he looked from us to the Orcas to Hernandez and back several times as he formulated his next question. "They came to you for help?"

"That's right, sir. We were fishing about a mile from here out in the Strait when the big female," I pointed to Mother over in the cove, "came to us and asked us to help them."

"How?"

"Well, sir, you are never going to believe it."

"Why don't you tell us over coffee? Follow me." He said as he led us down into the Cutter.

Explaining The Situation

So, we told him and Lieutenant Hernandez what had happened while some of the crew listened from the outside. "The pod mother, at least that is who we think she is, came out into the Strait and bumped our boat to get our attention. I could feel something like when Jill sends to me, so I touched the Orca and began receiving telepathic messages from her."

"Telepathic messages?" Captain Miller asked, a bewildered look on his face. "Telepathically? Like psychics?" He continued.

"Yes, sir," Jill replied. "Jack and I discovered we were mutually telepathic years ago, but 'hearing' the Orcas was a complete surprise to us."

"They seem to welcome your presence, considering how they are helping you get around. There is nothing to indicate they feel

23

threatened by you; in fact, quite the opposite, and I doubt that you have done any real harm except to the No-Contact Law." Captain Miller said.

"You actually spoke to the Orcas?" Lt. Hernandez asked.

"Yes, ma'am, we did." Jill said.

"Telepathically?"

"Yes, and no," I interjected. "I know that is no answer to your question. So let me explain. I suppose you might say that Jill and I are amateur psychics, but the reality is we have none of the perceptive abilities that psychics are said to have. We are mutually telepathic. To our delight, we found this out on our honeymoon and have had great fun with it over the years. We can't read minds, not even each other's minds. What we do is like talking, except we do it silently; we think things to each other. After teaching college for a couple of years, we decided to try show business as so-called mentalists, but we didn't have the gift for gab that show business psychics and mentalists have to have in order to convince the public that they are not faking it and believe me they are, faking it, that is. In our case, the people thought we were faking it somehow when in fact, we were the only honest mentalists in the show. So after a while, when it didn't work out, we went back to teaching. Concerning communicating with the Orcas, we were as surprised as you are."

"I doubt that." Captain Miller said.

I finished with, "And, Captain, I promised we would be here tomorrow to see how things are going."

"Okay, okay. We'll report you as animal rights and health researchers working closely with the Orcas. And, as required by law, I've already notified the Washington Department of Fish and Wildlife, the National Oceanic and Atmospheric Administration, and our headquarters that you are here. I'll follow up with a report that you are working closely with the Orcas to help an injured juvenile. You can bet someone is bound to show up to investigate."Then he added after some thought, "I think we'd better stand by to field the complaints and warn them off."

"Thank you, sir, that's a good idea. Could you please have your crew ferry us back to our boat?"

Before returning to our boat, Captain Miller suggested that we stay anchored where we were until the next day so we could be near the whales. The Coasties also offered us some provisions, which Jill gratefully accepted as we had only prepared for a day of fishing, not an extended voyage. As the whaleboat pulled away from the Cutter, Captain Miller stood on the foredeck, watching us and shaking his head in disbelief. Then, he threw us a salute before going back inside the Cutter.

Game Wardens Arrive

About an hour later, a WDFW Zodiac boat came roaring up. As promised, Captain Miller stopped them before they got too close. He presumably suggested that they approach our boat at trolling speed to avoid alarming the orcas. He must have told them some of what we had been doing because the Zodiac approached very slowly and coasted the last 20 yards with the motors off. There were two WDFW wardens in the Zodiac. The older one, a man, tossed us a line that Jill caught and used to pull them in and made fast to a cleat.

As I helped the warden come aboard our boat, he gave me a funny look and introduced himself. "Hi, I'm Tom Broderick, Supervisory Game Warden. What is going on?" Before I could answer, he added, "The Coast Guard Captain told us briefly what you were doing and explained that the wild Orcas were working with you or you were working with them. Is that right?"

Tom was the color of mahogany with short grey curly hair. He was shorter than me, probably in his mid-50s, and getting slightly paunchy. His handshake was firm but friendly.

"Hi, Tom, I am Jack Kline, and this is my wife Jill, and it is true."

"Jack and Jill, huh, eh convenient; how did you do it?" He asked Jill with a smile.

"Actually, neither one of us did it," Jill replied. "My given name is Dolores, but friends christened me Jill shortly after Jack and I began dating, and it stuck."

"Terrific. That's the best kind of nickname, Jill."

We heard a cough from the Zodiac, which caused Tom to turn his head. "Where are my manners? This is my assistant, Shirley White."

"Hi, Shirley," Jill said, offering Shirley her hand helped her aboard. Shirley was beautiful in an understated way, perhaps in her early 30s, probably a little younger than Jill. She had beautiful red hair cut short and curly and the golden complexion that true redheads so often have, and she looked great in her uniform.

Tom said, then, "What is the deal with the Orcas?"

"What Captain Miller told you is true; we have been working with the Orcas since earlier today." I answered, then added, "We have four seats in the boat for when we take friends fishing with us, but as you can see, it gets very crowded with four people all standing in the cockpit. So, let's sit down. Why don't you and Shirley take the two aft swivel seats, and we will flip the backs of the front seats to face you?

"Would you like a cold drink?" I asked.

"Thank you, no," Tom replied. "Now, please fill us in on what's going on."

I told them exactly the same thing we had told Captain Miller. They looked doubtful and started to ask questions about the situation.

"Mister Broderick," Jill interrupted before he could get started.

"Call me Tom," Broderick interrupted.

"Okay, Tom, I think it might be easier if we showed you." I 'heard' Jill call to the Orcas, [Mother, come] as she said it aloud.

Immediately, Mother swam out to the boat and bumped the side gently while sending a [?].

Jill reached out and stroked Mother's brow. "Tom and Shirley, this is Mother. She is the pod leader and the mother of the injured juvenile."

Broderick jumped to his feet, but before he could say or do anything, Shirley asked, "She lets you touch her? Is it safe?"

"It's quite safe," Jill replied. "She won't hurt you, but move slowly until she gets to know you."

Tom sat down again, looking both very confused and very doubtful. He cautioned, "Watch out, Shirley, they can be dangerous. One of them killed someone a few years ago."

"I read about that, Tom," Shirley replied. "She was a trainer for captive Orcas. But, as I recall, there is no reported incident of a wild Orca attacking a human."

Shirley stood, slowly held out her hand, and, in a calm and re-laxed tone, asked Jill, "Will she let me touch her?"

Tom started to say something, but I put my hand on his arm and shook my head at him. He stopped and looked at me out of the corner of his eye and shrugged. I smiled at him and whispered, "Wait!"

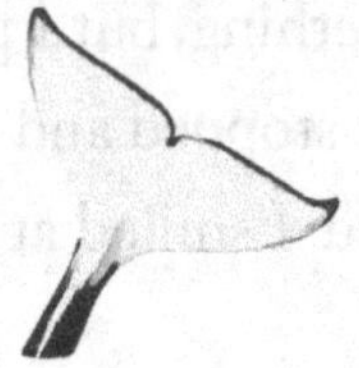

A New Friend

Jill asked Mother, [New Friend?] while looking at Shirley and sending soothing feelings. I translated for Tom's benefit and gave him a running narrative of everything that was happening.

Mother reared out of the water sky-scoping, looked over the side of the boat at Shirley and Tom, and replied with a single low click while, again, sending a [?].

"Mother wants to know why a new friend," I said.

Jill took Shirley's hand and guided it slowly towards Mother. Mother continued to project the question but held still as Jill placed Shirley's hand on Mother's brow. Mother paused for a moment and then moved slowly from side to side, clicking quietly as Shirley gently touched her.

Mother bumped Shirley's hand in return, then sent [Yes!]

"Mother accepts Shirley," I told Tom.

"She accepts you, Shirley," Jill said, smiling.

"I felt it," Shirley replied. "I felt it. It was like a wave of trust or love or something like what sometimes happens when you meet some strangers."

"I'll be a…" Tom began and then sat shaking his head in disbelief. "Can I…?"

"Not yet, Tom," Jill replied to his implied question. "She senses some hostility or distrust in you. Give her and yourself some time. She needs help, and she needs to trust us. I mean all of us who will be working on this. Trust her, and she will trust you."

"Okay," Tom conceded. "Somehow, I feel it will be worth the wait. How bad do you think the injury is?"

"I saw a couple of cuts and a nick across the top of the tail. The bigger cut, which is furthest from the flukes, might go down to the muscle, but the smaller cuts are superficial, just a bit more than skin deep. The biggest problem is, his back is sprained, and some skin was gouged out near his tail, leaving a hole." I replied.

"Fixable?" Tom asked, then frowned when he realized what he had asked.

"The right veterinarian with the right equipment could stitch up the cuts. However, there's no way to immobilize the Orca while doing the sutures, so it could very well be dangerous. We can try to calm him. I'm sure Mother and the other females will help once we communicate what's to be done. At the moment, the wounds are not bleeding freely, just seeping a little. The saltwater has probably helped that along with their natural healing abilities.

The Veterinarian

"Hmm," Tom thought for a minute, obviously considering what he wanted to say, then said, "I know a veterinarian who has worked with seals and dolphins. He's down at The Oregon Institute of Marine Studies in Portland. Let me see if I can contact him and find out what he thinks we should do."

"That would be great, Tom," Jill said.

Tom hopped back into the Zodiac and called WDFW Headquarters on the radio to report in and give them an assessment of the situation. He explained the problem in generalities and asked if he could call the veterinarian. After a five-minute heated discussion mostly about who would pay for it, he was reluctantly given permission to contact the vet. Instead of the radio, Tom used his cell phone to call the Institute in Portland. Ten more minutes of repeated vague descriptions and evasive explanations finally resulted in a connection to the veterinarian. After describing the problem without revealing everything that had happened, he turned to me and spoke loudly because he was still in the Zodiac more than a few feet away. "Jack, he says he might be able to help, but it will take him 6 hours or so to get here, and by then, it will be dark. What do you think? Can we put it off until tomorrow?"

As Tom was conversing with headquarters and the veterinarian, the Cutter drifted closer to us and was just twenty feet away as Tom was talking to the vet. Before we could answer, Captain Miller interrupted. "I heard that. Hang on folks; I may have a solution. Give me a minute."

"Hang on, Adrian; the Coast Guard Captain is checking something," Tom said.

Captain Miller did some quick radio work on the Coast Guard frequency, paused listening for a few minutes, spoke briefly, and asked. "Tom, how soon can the veterinarian be ready to leave and go over to the University Hospital helipad?"

Tom passed on the question to the veterinarian, listened for a moment, then told Captain Miller, "Sir, he asks if twenty minutes will be okay, and can he bring a graduate assistant with him?"

Captain Miller again spent a couple of minutes talking on the radio, then he said, "Tell him a Coast Guard rescue chopper will pick them up in twenty minutes, that is them, plural. Okay?"

Tom repeated the message to the veterinarian, listened a moment, then told us, "He says they'll be waiting, Captain."

"Great!" Captain Miller said. "It should take them less than two hours to pick up the vet and his helper and bring them up here. Now, what do we do?"

The Cutter was still drifting closer to us with the tide. "First, I suggest you keep the cutter away from our boat so the Orcas don't get nervous," I replied.

He nodded in agreement and spoke quietly to Lt. Hernandez, who spoke to the woman at the controls. The Cutter backed away about 50 yards and anchored.

Then I said to Jill and the wardens. "Now, I guess the best thing we can do is get back in the water and try to explain the whole thing to Mother and Sonny. So let's zip up and get to it, Jill."

"How cold is the water?" Shirley asked.

"Not too bad," I replied. "It is probably in the mid-sixties."

"Can I come too?" Shirley asked, "I have a wet suit, and I took a Reiki class several years ago. In fact, I was trying to send energy to Mother when I touched her."

"That explains why she accepted you so quickly. I'm not too sure she can tell us apart." Jill said.

"She can tell you apart," I interjected. "I could tell when you introduced Shirley that Mother knew Shirley was someone different, and she trusted her because we did."

Jill considered Shirley's request, then said, "Come if you want to, but if you spook him, you'll have to back away. There is no way to force them to accept you. Mother seems to think you're okay, and I think she's the boss. But Sonny is or was very upset and stressed. Stress and fear are the main problems."

Getting into a wet suit is never a fast process, but Shirley shucked her uniform down to her panties and bra and wriggled into her wet suit in under five minutes. The fact that several men were watching her in amazement didn't bother her until she looked around as she zipped up and blushed bright red, then bowed while the men, including me, applauded.

Jill sat up on the gunnel and invited Shirley to sit beside her. Jill explained again about the ride with the Orcas.

"Ready?" Jill asked.

Shirley nodded assent, and together they rolled backward into the water.

"The water's not too bad at all," Shirley exclaimed. "I'm surprised."

I stood up to follow them, but Jill held up her hand and said, "Why don't you hang here with Tom, Jack and just let us go alone, for starters."

"Good idea," I replied and sat back down with Tom.

Mother was still nearby, and once the two women were in the water, she called out to the pod for help. In seconds, two large male Orcas swam over to give Jill and Shirley a ride. Tom started to get up and say something, but I held him down and said, "Relax, Tom, it'll be okay, trust me."

"I…," Tom started so say.

Trust me," I repeated.

Tom looked doubtful but nodded assent.

Jill explained to Shirley what was going to happen. "Swim away from the boat and just tread water. In a minute or so, those two

Orcas will swim around behind us and give us a ride over to the injured Orca. Just grasp the dorsal fin as it swims behind and up under you to push."

"Okay, I'll follow your lead," Shirley replied.

In less than a minute, they were ferried over to Sonny on the backs of the Orcas. Jill told me later that Mother soothed Sonny and told him that Shirley was okay. Shirley swam slowly up to Sonny, and while Jill comforted him, Shirley looked at the wounds. Then, she very carefully reached out to touch Sonny; he flinched at the touch of an unfamiliar hand but not as violently as he did when I first touched him. Within a few moments, Sonny accepted Shirley as she gently ran her hands over the affected area.

Jill and Mother discussed what would happen when the veterinarian arrived and reassured her that she and Shirley would be there to help.

The Orcas brought Jill and Shirley back to our boat when they finished with Sonny. Tom and I helped them back aboard.

Shirley was positively beaming when she was seated again. "That was incredible, Tom; you have no idea. I was scared when he flinched, but as soon as I stroked him gently, Mother talked to him, and he relaxed." Then she told me, "As you guessed, his cuts don't look too serious, but they could use some treatment to prevent serious infection and promote healing. Given time, they would probably heal anyway, but it might be a problem for him. The gouge and the sprain, on the other hand, are probably very painful, and I have no idea what can be done about that."

Tom just sat there at a loss for words, as Shirley reported. Finally, he leaned back in the chair and, with a shrug, nodded and smiled in accepting disbelief, then said, "Shirley, I am incredibly proud of you. If I hadn't seen it, I would never believe it, and I don't think anyone else will either."

We sat and talked about what to do for the next hour while we munched on some of the snacks the Coast Guard had provided. While we waited, a smaller Coast Guard launch arrived from the Port Angeles Coast Guard Station and moored with the Cutter. Before long we heard the familiar whup-whup-whup of an approaching helicopter and looked up to see the unmistakable White, International Orange, and Black of a Coast Guard Rescue Helicopter. It landed on the afterdeck helipad of the Cutter and disembarked the two Oregon Institute scientists and their gear. They spoke briefly with Captain Miller, who led them down the ladder into the launch, which ferried them over to us.

"May I suggest that we use the launch as our base of operations in the cove? Unfortunately, Jack, your boat is too small to accommodate all of us, and the Zodiac can't hold more than three or four." Captain Miller suggested when they arrived. So, we all moved to the launch.

Meet Dr. Goodhurst

Tom Broderick performed the introductions; Jack and Jill Kline; this is my brother-in-law, Dr. Adrian Goodhurst, and his assistant. Adrian, you've met Shirley before at our house, of course.

Dr. Goodhurst, a tall and slender individual with thinning hair, said, "Hello all, please call me Adrian. This is my graduate assistant and, as her t-shirt says, an aspiring marine veterinarian, Chloe Crocker."

Chloe stood and greeted us. She was dressed like a typical college student in jeans and a t-shirt emblazoned with 'I like sea critters.' She was taller than average and nearly as slender as Adrian. Her hair was blond with a ponytail; she had freckles on her nose, and she had a whimsical smile. She blushed and said, "Hi, I'm so excited to be here."

Then Adrian provided the rest of the introductions, "You all know Captain Miller, and this is Senior Chief Lemuel Greene." he said, indicating the launch coxswain, who nodded in greeting. Then he continued, now, can you tell me the details of what this is all about? All I know so far is that an injured juvenile Orca needs help."

Once again, we told our story to an amazed audience. Adrian looked inquiringly at Tom and asked with a raised eyebrow. "Tom?"

"I saw it with my own eyes, Adrian. Of course, I wouldn't have believed it either, but I saw it, or I would never have called you." Tom replied.

"Okay, let's say I believe you. Now what do you suggest?"

"Shirley thinks we may need to do something to prevent a serious infection and maybe some stitches for the cuts," Tom replied.

Shirley filled in the details, "The cuts are still oozing some blood, not a lot, but some. The largest cut could probably use some stitches if he stands still for it. There is a gouge out of his back about the size of my hand" she said, holding up her hand, "and it's bleeding more than the cuts, and, in my opinion, his back is definitely sprained, and it hurts him a lot, he can hardly move his tail. Jack and Jill gave him Healing Hands energy healing when they first arrived, and then Jill and I gave more while we were waiting for you to arrive. That seemed to calm him down considerably. He is or was pretty relaxed at the moment."

Adrian's eyebrows went up at the mention of Healing Hands, but he said nothing. Finally, after a few moments of thought, he said, "It's too late today to do much except maybe give him a broad-spectrum antibiotic. Trying to do stitches in the dark on a large animal is not a good idea, no matter how calm it may seem to be. How thick is the blubber in the area of the wounds?"

"A couple of inches, I would guess," Shirley replied. "What would you say, Jill?"

"Shirley has given a good assessment of the situation." Jill concurred.

"Would either of you feel comfortable giving him a shot?" Adrian asked the girls. "I ask because you have been working with him, and from what you say, he seems to know and trust you."

"How much is it likely to hurt him?" Jill asked.

"Well, I have never given a shot to an Orca, but I have to dolphins when they were held motionless in a harness. Of course, they didn't like it, but after the first one, they seemed to accept it." Adrian replied.

"Senior Chief, would you please take us back to the cutter so we can get to our equipment and supplies?" Adrian asked.

"Yes, sir," Senior Chief Greene replied as he started the engine and drove us over to the Cutter.

When we arrived at the Cutter, we all went aboard.

"Go get my bag, please, Chloe," Adrian said.

Chloe fetched what looked much like any other doctor's large valise and handed it to Adrian, who quickly searched through it and found what was needed. He handed the bottle of antibiotics to Chloe, who was preparing the hypodermics while Jill and Shirley watched.

"How big is the needle?" Jill asked as she saw Chloe filling the hypodermic.

Chloe held the hypodermic up so Jill could see it and said, "I would guess it is about the size of the lead in a wooden pencil, 14 gauge."

"Good Lord, that is huge," Jill exclaimed. "I'd better go over there alone to do this."

"No way," Shirley said, "I'm going too. Maybe I can comfort him while you explain to Mother what is going to happen so she can explain it to Sonny first."

Jill looked relieved at Shirley's offer. "We'd better do it tonight so he has time to get over it before we try stitching him up."

"Can I come too?" Chloe asked.

"No!" Jill and Shirley replied in chorus. Jill explained, "He knows us, Chloe. Trying to introduce someone new at the same time we're giving the shot is probably not a good idea. I haven't figured out yet how to explain to Mother what we'll be doing. Just finish getting the hypodermic ready, and Shirley and I will give it a try."

Chloe looked disappointed but prepared what looked like a huge hypodermic with the antibiotic. When she finished, Adrian suggested to her, "Give them a hypo with some Lidocaine to numb the site before giving him the antibiotic. That should help to make it as painless as possible."

Jill looked expectantly at Chloe, who replied, "A much smaller needle for the Lidocaine. Inject it first and then give it a few minutes to work before injecting the antibiotic."

"Okay," Shirley replied as she accepted the hypodermics from Chloe, who had placed them in a plastic bag to keep them dry and sterile as long as possible.

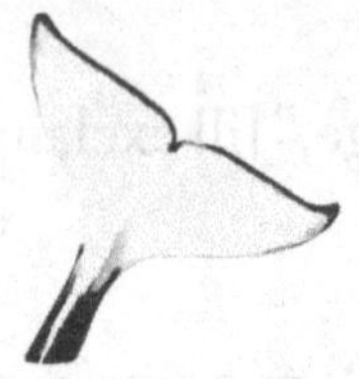

Inoculating Sonny

A few minutes later, as sunset approached, Jill and Shirley again entered the water. Jill called [Mother] and began to swim toward the Orcas. Almost immediately, two of the Orcas swam over to tow them back into the cove where the pod was waiting.

As the Orcas were towing them over to where Sonny was resting, Adrian said, "If I hadn't seen this, I would not have believed it. Does Jill actually talk to the pod Mother?"

"Yes, and no," I replied. "Jill 'thinks' the idea to Mother, who is the best communicator in the pod at the moment. She only says it aloud for us to hear what she is saying and to help her formulate the message correctly."

"Are you saying she does it psychically?" Adrian asked.

"More like telepathically," I replied.

"How? What's the difference?"

"It's nearly impossible to explain how we do it; we just do. Jill is more able to communicate with animals on some level than I am. She regularly goes over to the Humane Society and helps to calm the dogs, and some of the cats, but cats are a whole different problem." I rambled on, "She doesn't communicate with the dogs the same way she does with the Orcas. But, understand, connecting with the Orcas was a complete surprise to both of us. If the Orcas hadn't tried to communicate with us, we would never have known it was possible. We knew Orcas, porpoises, dolphins, and whales were very intelligent with large, well-developed brains, but like everybody else, we thought they just communicated with clicks, squeaks, tones, whale songs and the like. Now, I'm convinced that they are telepathic and able to communicate that way as well. I think many of the clicks and other noises might be just punctuation or perhaps longer-range communications. I'm pretty sure that the clicks can travel farther than the telepathy, but I wouldn't bet on it."

Adrian just sat staring at me as if I was spouting heresy. Then he began to nod his head slowly as he absorbed what I was telling him. As I've learned over my years as a teacher, learning something that contradicts everything you thought you knew is never pleasant or easy. But, in this case, the evidence was right here to be seen.

Mother's Surprise

The water in the cove was dead flat; there was no wind, not even a breeze, so I could overhear Jill speaking while she communicated telepathically, and we could hear them both as they spoke aloud. I could also receive Mother's messages to Jill, which I vocalized for the benefit of everyone. Jill did most of the talking while Shirley focused on soothing Sonny. Jill showed Mother the hypodermics and tried to explain what they wanted to do would help make Sonny well again. Then, Mother surprised us all.

[Me, first,] was the gist of her request.

Jill and Shirley talked it over and concluded that since the site on Sonny could not be made sterile, it probably would not make much difference if they used the needles on Mother first. As they talked, Chloe filled another syringe with Lidocaine, put it in a bag, dove into the water, clothes and all, and began swimming towards the pod. As she approached the pod, she shouted, "To try it on Mother first, you will probably use up the Lidocaine to numb her. So I'm bringing another Lidocaine syringe for Sonny."

Jill and Shirley immediately understood and explained what Chloe was doing to Mother. Then, almost on cue, the 'Orca Express' was dispatched to bring Chloe over to the pod. Chloe could not keep from shouting "Awesome" as she was being ferried over to the pod on the back of an Orca.

Once Chloe was with them, Jill invited Chloe to do the injections since she had the most experience. That left Jill and Shirley free to soothe and comfort Sonny while Chloe injected one of the Lidocaine hypos into Mother's back in about the same place on her as they would be injected into Sonny. After she gave the Lidocaine a couple of minutes to work, she plunged the larger needle onto Mother without injecting the antibiotic. Mother had been prepared as much as possible, and she didn't even flinch, that we could see. Then through Jill, I overheard and repeated aloud what Mother told Sonny was going to happen and that he should stay still when they did it.

Jill later told us that despite the healing treatments we had given him earlier, Sonny was still in enough pain from his injuries that any pains from the needle sticks were virtually lost in the process. As far as Jill could tell, he didn't feel them, although he did flinch when the bigger needle was inserted, more because of the pressure in a tender area than because of the injection itself. When they finished injecting Sonny, the three women were ferried back to the Cutter.

When they arrived back at the Cutter, Chloe was the first one aboard. She immediately began to tell Adrian and the rest of us about what had happened. "You are never going to believe it, Adrian. He hardly moved. When I finished, Mother gave me a gentle nudge which Jill said was a show of appreciation." Chloe fairly glowed as she told us about her experience as Jill and Shirley were being helped back aboard.

When she ran out of things to tell us, Adrian asked, "Aren't you cold, Chloe?"

"I am now with these wet clothes out here in the open," she replied. "But the water wasn't as cold as I've experienced elsewhere. I'm sorry I didn't bring even a windbreaker or a coat, but how could I know?"

As she was telling her story, the crew of the Cutter was listening. When she finished, Senior Chief Greene offered a solution. "We always have a few extra jumpsuits aboard the Cutter because we often get wet doing our jobs. We have three women aboard, and one of them might be able to find you a jumpsuit."

"Thank you, sir, I would really appreciate that," Chloe replied.

Senior Chief Greene looked at her and started to say something when Captain Miller interjected, "Chloe, the proper way to address a Chief Petty Officer is not sir; it is Chief or, in this case, Senior Chief."

"I'm sorry, Senior Chief," Chloe said with a sheepish smile.

"No harm done, miss. It's a common mistake among the "uninitiated." Greene said, a twinkle in his eye. "Go with Petty Officer Grey. I am sure she can find something that will fit, more or less."

"Senior Chief," Jill said, "would you mind running us back over to our boat so Shirley, Jack, and I can get out of these wetsuits and back into dry clothes?"

"Can do!" Senior Chief Greene replied.

Before we descended the ladder into the launch, Captain Miller said, "Why don't you just pick up your clothes and bring them back here to the Cutter? We have a locker room where you can change out of the wetsuits and even shower if you want to. In addition, I spoke to Lieutenant Hernandez, and she has invited you all to have dinner with us and sleep aboard the Cutter tonight, where I am sure you will be much more comfortable than on either your boat or the Zodiac."

Aboard the Cutter

When we returned to the Cutter with dry clothes on, the sun was setting, and an evening breeze was cooling the area.

Lieutenant Hernandez greeted us as we climbed aboard. "Ladies, if you will follow First Class Willson, she will show you to the locker room and help Chloe find a clean jumpsuit. Mr. Kline, after the ladies are finished, you may use the locker room and shower as well. Unfortunately, we only have one small locker room and shower, so we have to take turns. You will be sleeping in crew bunks if that is okay."

"No problem, ma'am," Jill spoke for all the ladies, "but if we sleep in crew bunks, where will the crew sleep?"

"Jill, please call me Juanita. As for the bunks, we're used to roughing it. There are not enough bunks for everybody, so only half the crew can sleep in a bunk at any one time anyway. So on nights like this, when it's warm, and there's no wind, some of us sleep in sleeping bags on the deck."

"Thank you, Juanita," Jill said with a nod as she, Shirley, and Chloe followed First Class Willson down into the locker room.

"Lieutenant, er Juanita," I said, "I'll shower later, but I would like to get out of this wetsuit."

"No problem, Mr. Kline; you can use my cabin to change and wash up using the sink." Lieutenant Hernandez replied.

"It's Jack, Juanita; Mr. Kline was my father; I'm just Jack," I said.

"Yes, sir, Jack. Please follow me." She said as she led me to her cabin, which was about the size of a small walk-in closet. "The sink folds down under the mirror, and the toilet is under the sink which folds up out of the way should you need it."

After we had all redressed, we were invited into the crew's mess for dinner. The room was stuffed to overflow with Captain Miller, Lieutenant Hernandez, the two helicopter pilots, Tom and Shirley, Adrian and Chloe, and Jill and me. Chloe had returned dressed in a jumpsuit at least two sizes too big for her with rolled-up sleeves and cuffs. But she was grinning from ear to ear. Dinner was sandwiches, coffee, tea or milk, and some cookies that one of the crew had cobbled up during the day for the occasion.

Evidence Arrives

We had just finished dinner when we were interrupted by Willson, "Skipper, she said to Lieutenant Hernandez, we just got a text from Port Angeles telling you to look on your tablet; there is something you need to see. They said it's on your tablet too, Captain Miller."

"Thanks, Willson," Lieutenant Hernandez said as she and Captain Miller took their tablets and activated them.

Hernandez received the message first, opened it, and exclaimed, "Oh my God! Hang on, everybody, I'll put this up on the big screen."

We all turned to look at the large screen at the back of the room that doubled as a television and communal computer monitor. What showed was a video of a small blue and white fishing boat racing along at such a high speed that it was skipping from wavelet to wavelet. It was heading from left to right across the screen. A pod of Orcas was at the far right side of the screen. A few seconds later, the boat turned toward the Orcas, who dove to get out of the way. At that moment, a smaller Orca surfaced for air, and the boat turned directly toward it. A second later, the boat hit the small Orca behind the dorsal fin so hard that the boat bounced into the air. Then the boat sped off and kept going.

Lieutenant Hernandez continued, "According to a longer email that followed the video, the video was taken by one of the volunteers who monitor the Orcas and record their activities. The volunteer was on a bluff on the south side of the Strait, almost due southwest of here. According to the person who took the call at the station, the woman who recorded it was sobbing and cursing in the background as her husband explained what happened. The husband said that his wife's friend used binoculars and was pretty sure that the boat's name started with an 'S', but the trolling motor blocked the rest. They also noticed, as can be seen, that the driver was wearing a blue hat and the passenger was wearing a blue hat, and worst of all, the driver made a gesture indicating he was proud of what he had done. Did any of you notice that or should I play the video again?"

The mess was dead quiet as we all processed what we had seen. Then several people, including Tom and Shirley, commented that they had seen the hats and the gesture.

"Well, there's our smoking gun," Captain Miller said. "The only problem is, there must be a gazillion blue and white fishing boats plying the Strait. It doesn't look like the video is good enough for an analyst to get the name of the boat or the faces of the people in it. So without a credible witness, what can we do?"

"If they went by here once, they are sure to go by again, but as you said, blue and white boats are a dime a dozen around here, but we can at least eliminate those with outboard motors; that boat has an inboard engine." I said, then added, "I'd say it looked like an eighteen or twenty-foot Arima, which should also serve to narrow the search."

"Good eye, Jack." Captain Miller said. "But even if we stopped every blue and white Arima inboard fishing boat, without some corroborating evidence, how could we prove which one did it? The possibility of the name beginning with an 'S' might be some help, but we would still be shooting in the dark with the possible exception of the hats."

"Well, let's get on with what we can do. Adrian, you're the Doctor; what should we plan on doing in the morning?" I asked.

"I'd like to go over and take a look at the injuries before I decide. We should stitch up the propellor cuts if for no other reason than to minimize the chances of infection. As for the piece that was gouged out of his back, I'm not sure how to handle that. It might be possible to sterilize the wound site and pull it closed with stitches, but the way Shirley described it, I doubt it. On the other hand, if I had the missing piece, I might be able to stitch it over the wound like a skin graft."

"Adrian, that gouge is pretty deep, maybe an inch or more." Jill offered.

"I have some surgical foam in my case. We use it to pack wounds or fill a hole sometimes where tissue is lost before we do a skin graft. The foam slowly dissolves and allows the body to replace it with new tissue. It isn't perfect, but it is a lot better than just stretching a piece of skin over the wound or, even worse, leaving the wound open. I'll have to see the wound to be sure. Then I have the problem of immobilizing him while I am doing the surgery. Anesthesia is not a good idea because we cannot easily predict how long he would be unconscious. Plus, there is some risk that his natural breathing during his sleep cycle would be disrupted, and he might not be able to breathe normally and might drown. We might be able to beach him, but that would probably put his tail underwater, and besides, having him out of the water for any amount of time would probably not be too healthy either."

Jill thought for a moment and said, "Adrian, with Mother nearby like she was today, we would probably be okay doing the stitching without Lidocaine because the pain of the wounds will probably mask the stitching process. If he flinches, we can always inject the local anesthesia before proceeding."

Shirley added, "He didn't even flinch when Chloe gave him the shots."

"Okay, that settles it then." Adrian took charge. "But, I should be the one to do the stitching, not because any of you couldn't do a credible job, but because I'll need you to keep him calm while I do it."

"Agreed," Jill and Shirley said. Chloe was disappointed but agreed.

Once those decisions were made, the discussion became more personal as we interacted with some of the crew and each other. While Tom and Shirley discussed with Captain Miller what they should do about the whole situation, Jill and I befriended Adrian and Chloe. However, it was a non-event with Chloe, who just sat there soaking up the conversations and eye-flirting with the helicopter pilots and some of the men in the crew.

After a bit, Adrian took a different tack, "Healing Hands, huh? I've heard about it but don't know anything about it. It seems to me that most of the traditional medical profession sort of discounts the effects, I think mainly because they can't regulate or control it. So I wonder, could I learn how to do it?"

"Are you aware that Healing Hands was used extensively on the battlefield in the middle east and that some hospitals have instituted a Healing Hands program with their nursing staff?" Jill asked.

"No, I was not aware of either of those things. So how would one go about learning it?"

"Easy," Jill replied, "there are undoubtedly lots of practitioners in the Portland area, and where there are practitioners, there are training sessions. It takes about three sessions to become a novice, but believe you, me, you will know it even after one session; the rest is just practice."

"Lieutenant Hernandez, excuse me, Juanita, we girls are pretty tired. Could we turn it in now?" Shirley asked.

"Certainly, Shirley. Can you find your way, or would you like a guide?"

"We only need a guide to tell us if any particular bunk is assigned to someone here. We don't want to tread on anyone's toes."

"The bunks are all first come, first served. So just pick one that suits you."

"Thanks, good night all. Coming Jill, Chloe?" Shirley asked

"May I stay up for a while? I'm not tired yet." Chloe asked.

"Suit yourself," Jill replied, yawning, as she followed Shirley down into the bunk room.

Tom, Captain Miller, Adrian, and I sat up chatting for a while, then turned in for the night. When we went down to the bunk room, Chloe and Willson were still engaged in a running chat session with the men. Lieutenant Hernandez turned her cabin over to Captain Miller and curled up in her command chair. I snuggled in behind Jill on one of the bunks.

Treating Sonny

In the morning, after a breakfast of toast and pop tarts, Jill and Shirley doned their wetsuits and went over to check things out and to explain to Mother what was going to happen. I relayed Mother's reactions to the rest of the party. Jill reported that Sonny seemed relaxed after his Mother explained things to him while Jill and Shirley gave him Healing Hands to help keep him calm.

When they were sure Sonny was ready, Jill waved for Adrian and Chloe to come and join them. Adrian had borrowed Tom's wetsuit, which was too big, but it was all that was available. Chloe came on deck wearing a t-shirt over her underwear. Several Orcas were waiting to ferry them over to Sonny when they entered the water. When they arrived in the cove, Jill introduced Adrian to Mother, and he acted as if he did this sort of thing every day. He stroked her head and spoke to her as if she could understand him, and Jill announced that Mother accepted him.

"I learned a long time ago that most animals will accept you if you approach them slowly, you are calm, and you speak quietly to them. But I wouldn't want to try that on a lion or tiger, thank you very much." Adrian said.

While Adrian checked the injuries, Jill and Shirley continued calming Sonny and describing what was happening to Mother. The ladies continued to soothe Sonny to keep him calm while Adrain and Chloe injected the anesthetic and gave it a few minutes to work before proceeding with the stitching. Sonny wiggled some but kept as still as could be expected during the process. When they finished, the Orcas escorted them back to the Cutter.

Once we were all back together, Adrian asked, "We've done all we can do. Can we stay for a while, Captain? We'd like to see how it goes."

Captain Miller conferred briefly with the helicopter pilots and reported, "The chopper doesn't have to return right away, so sure, you can stay as long as you like. Besides, Chloe appears to have the pilots enthralled."

"Yeah, she tends to do that," Adrian said, smiling and shaking his head. "You wouldn't know it to look at her. Don't misunderstand, she is cute and all, but whatever else it is, she has IT!"

We all smiled and nodded in agreement.

Adrian and Chloe stayed with us through the morning to observe Sonny. By noon Sonny was swimming slowly around the cove and seemed much better. Adrian went back into the cove to examine Sonny and was satisfied that the stitches were holding, then returned to the Cutter.

"I guess we can leave now, Captain Miller. Except for the gouge, everything seems to be all right with the Orcas." Adrian said, "Tom, when are you and my sister going to come down to Portland for a visit?"

"I need to stay here until the fishing season is over; after that, we'll give you a call and drop down your way."

"See you then, and by all means, bring Shirley," Adrian said as he and Chloe went aft to board the idling helicopter.

That's The Boat

Tom and Shirley were preparing to leave in their Zodiac when a blue and white inboard fishing boat came tearing down the Strait at full throttle, headed west. Immediately, three of the larger male Orcas sky-scoped, looking at the boat, and then took off after it.

Mother swam over to our boat and lifted her head above the water. [Boat hurt Sonny!]

[That boat?] Jill asked aloud.

[Yes!] Mother exclaimed, then sent Jill an image of the boat streaming away after it hit Sonny. The image was clearer than before, and the name on the stern was legible.

"Captain, please stop the helicopter," Jill shouted, then added, "Tom, Mother says that was the boat that hit Sonny. She sent me an Orca's eye image of it, and I could just barely make out the name 'Sally Sue' on the stern."

"Let's go, Shirley." Tom said, starting the Zodiac's motors, then to me, "Tell the Coasties we'll bring them back."

"Are you sure?" I asked.

"Oh, yeah, this thing can outrun everything but a hydroplane."

"Captain, you heard?" I shouted to Captain Miller.

"I heard." He said, then signaled the helicopter pilots to stay aboard and radioed the situation to the base at Port Angeles. He thought for a moment, then said, "The cutter can't possibly catch them or keep up with the Zodiac or the fishing boat, so we will just wait here until Tom and Shirley get back."

"Captain," Lieutenant Hernandez said, "why don't we have the helicopter chase them too to make sure they don't get away."

"Great idea, Lieutenant." He replied, then waved to the helicopter pilots and signaled them to join the chase. Then he said to me, "Jack, can you ask Mother to call back the three Orcas that took off after the boat? We do not want any accusation of Orcas attacking humans and humans replying claiming self-defense."

Jill dove back into the water and swam over to Mother. I never did completely understand what she said. They were communicating on another level now. But when she returned to the Cutter, she reported. "Captain. She says she had already called them back when it was obvious they could not catch the boat. She also told them not to attack any boats either. That we had treated Sonny would take care of the problem."

"Really, all that?" Captain Miller asked.

"Well, not exactly word for word, sir." Jill replied, "But she understood what I was telling her and asking her to do, and because of how we treated Sonny, she was predisposed to let us take care of the problem."

Just then, the radio squawked with a call from the helicopter. "We've caught up to them and are blocking them from escaping while the Game Wardens have cornered them by Protection Island." A pause, "The Game Wardens have boarded their boat and have them under arrest. We're heading back. Out."

A little over an hour later, Tom drove the Zodiac back into the cove. Shirley followed in the 'Sally Sue.' Two handcuffed men, one wearing a blue hat and the other wearing a yellow hat, were sitting on the front seat of the Zodiac. The red Hat was protesting loudly, and the other sat quietly, shaking his head. When the protester looked up at the Cutter and saw Captain Miller, he started for the ladder and climbed aboard the Cutter, followed by his partner. Then he immediately demanded that they be released.

"Captain," he said, getting nose to nose with Captain Miller, "I don't know what sort of bogus accusations these guys have been feeding you, but we're just a pair of fishermen minding our own business, and we demand to be released immediately with a full apology."

Captain Miller ignored the demand and addressed Tom. "Did you Mirandize them, Tom?"

"Yes, sir, I told them they were under arrest and repeated the complete Miranda statement verbatim."

"Good! Then you realize that anything you say or do can be used as evidence in a court of law." Captain Miller asserted in a commanding voice. "What are your names?"

"Sam Gunderson and Charlie Morgenstern," the loudmouth announced.

"Who's who?"

"I'm Sam, and he's Charlie," Sam replied.

"Who owns the boat?"

"He does," Charlie said, pointing at Sam.

"If you are so innocent, why did you run away from the Game Wardens when they hailed you to stop?"

"I didn't know whether they wanted us or some other boat," Sam said. "There were other boats around, and we were in a hurry to get to our fishing spot."

"Tom?" Captain Miller asked the Game Warden.

"They were doing their best to get away once we hailed them and ordered them to stop. They cut across the shallows off Protection Island, hoping we wouldn't or couldn't follow. I guess they didn't know that a Zodiac only draws about six inches of water. They were obviously heading for shore, and presumably, a getaway until the helicopter blocked that. Eventually, we ran them down and cornered them against the island. We got it all on video, so they can protest all they want, but it won't help. Also, Captain, there were no other boats within hailing distance."

Captain Miller looked up at the two helicopter pilots who had just joined the group. "There were no other boats in sight, Captain." The pilot said.

"Did they say anything, Tom?"

"Yes, sir, they demanded; actually, it was that one," Tom said, pointing at Sam. "He demanded that we tell them why we arrested them and what they were being accused of."

"Yeah, Captain, what is it we done?" Sam interjected, still belligerent.

Before Captain Miller could answer, Tom added, indicating Sam, "He said that whatever we were accusing them of, they were innocent. Then he said he wanted a lawyer."

"He's going to need one," Captain Miller said. Then he confronted Sam directly. "Aside from resisting arrest and unlawful flight and, I'm sure, an assortment of violations on your boat, you are accused of running over an Orca with your boat two days ago."

"That's bull, Captain; there is no way that anyone can prove we ran over an Orca, and you can't search our boat; we know the law."

"That is what we are here to find out, Mr. Gunderson."

"Captain, this is what you asked for." Lieutenant Hernandez said, handing Captain Miller an official-looking document.

"Thank you, Lieutenant," he replied, then turned back to the two men, "this is an official search warrant for your boat and equipment. Lieutenant Hernandez, can you have their boat hoisted aboard the Cutter?"

"Yes, sir. Senior Chief, would you please hoist their boat aboard?"

"Yes, ma'am, Skipper, right away. You two come with me." Senior Chief Greene said, gathering two of the Cutter's crew with a nod.

"Lieutenant, may I speak to you for a minute, please?" Captain Miller asked Lieutenant Hernandez.

She nodded assent and led the way to the command deck. They spoke briefly then Captain Miller said, "Mr. Mortenstern, would you please go with Lieutenant Hernandez? She has some questions she would like to ask you."

"Yes, sir," Charlie answered, hanging his head and following Lieutenant Hernandez down the steps into the wardroom on the lower deck.

"Charlie, keep your mouth shut. Do you hear me? Tell them nothing! Nothing!" Sam shouted.

When they left, the rest of us stood quietly watching Senior Chief Greene and his team hoist the Sally Sue aboard the Cutter and leave her hanging from a davit on the port side.

"Ready, Captain." The Senior Chief said.

"Thank you, Senior Chief; now, would you search the boat for any violations of Coast Guard Regulations." Captain Miller ordered.

"Yes, sir, it would be a pleasure." Senior Chief Greene replied, gesturing to the two men who hoisted the 'Sally Sue' aboard.

"That's illegal search and seizure; you have no right to do that." Sam asserted.

"Did you read the search warrant when I gave it to you, Mr. Gunderson? It clearly states the boat is to be searched inside and out from stem to stern."

"That's bogus; you have to get a court order to do that," Sam mumbled.

"No, sir, Mr. Gunderson, the Coast Guard has the right to stop and search any boat in the water for violations of Coast Guard Regulations."

Fifteen minutes later, Senior Chief Greene returned with a clipboard. "Captain, this here," he said as he handed the clipboard to Captain Miller, "is a partial list of the violations. After I filled out this page, I quit. The whole damned boat is in violation of the Regulations."

"Why am I not surprised?" Captain Miller asked facetiously.

"Captain, do you mind if I take a look at the bottom of the boat? I want to see the keel?" Adrian asked.

"Please do, Dr. Goodhurst." Captain Miller replied.

The same three men went with Adrian to thoroughly search the bottom of the boat. A few minutes later, one of the men was heard to say. "Got it, Senior Chief."

Senior Chief Greene looked at what the man had found and said, "Show it to Dr. Goodhurst, Lewis."

Lewis handed the item he had found to Adrian, who looked it over carefully and then showed it to Captain Miller. "This is definitely a piece of Orca skin, Captain. Lewis found it wedged under one of the screws on the bottom of the boat."

Captain Miller examined a scrap of skin, nodded in agreement, and showed it to Sam. "I thought as much." He exclaimed. "This, Mr. Gunderson, is a piece of Orca skin with some of the flesh still attached. It was caught on one of the screws that hold the keel strip to the bottom of your boat."

"I could have picked that up anywhere; you might even have planted it," Gunderson said, looking at his feet; he refused to look at either the Captain or the piece of skin.

At that point, Lieutenant Hernandez returned and whispered in Captain Miller's ear.

"Anyway, you can't prove I hit an Orca. So I want a lawyer." Gunderson said.

"Actually, I can prove you hit the Orca, sir. Your friend Charlie told Lieutenant Hernandez the whole story, just how it happened, and signed an affidavit. I might also add there were other witnesses to the event who won't be needed now that we have Mr. Gunderson's testimony."

"What are you going to do to me?" Sam asked, somewhat subdued.

"We're going to impound your boat and all your equipment and take you with us to Port Angeles, where you will be arraigned before a federal judge for violations of Coast Guard Regulations and for deliberately interfering with or harming an Orca, which is a far more serious Federal offense. Orcas are protected under the Marine Mammal Protection Act, which is enforced by The National Oceanic and Atmospheric Administration and the Coast Guard at the Federal level and the Washington Department of Fish and

Wildlife at the State level. I suspect that in addition to losing your boat and paying a massive fine, you will be spending time in a Federal Penitentiary for breaking the laws designed to protect Orcas from just this sort of thing. Senior Chief Greene, would you please select a crew for the 'Sally Sue' and take Mr. Gunderson and Mr. Mortenstern to Port Angeles and hold them there in the brig until we return."

"With pleasure, sir. Lewis, please lower the 'Sally Sue' into the water and take the helm while we take these two to the brig in P. A."

"Aye, aye, Senior Chief," Lewis replied.

Patching Sonny

After Senior Chief Greene and Lewis departed for Port Angeles with the prisoners, Captain Miller turned to Adrian. "Well, Dr. Goodhurst, what do you think? Can you do anything with this piece of skin? It's pretty beat up and ragged." Captain Miller asked.

"Yes, sir, I think I can. As you suggest, it is not in the best possible condition, but it is thick and has several layers, and there is even some blubber remaining on the inside. Let me think about it for a minute or two." Adrian turned the piece of Orca skin over and over and tried to stretch it, then reported. "I think I can adapt this piece of skin along with some surgical foam and mesh to cover the hole. I'll use the foam mixed with some of the blubber to fill the hole."

"How can you do that considering its condition? Isn't it dead?" Captain Miller asked.

"Actually, the temperature of the water helped to partially preserve some of the viability of the specimen. Plastic surgeons have been experimenting with stretching a skin graft by making shallow parallel cuts just through the epidermis and other layers close to the surface. Then the graft is stretched perpendicular to the cuts, thus expanding and making the graft cover a larger area. It doesn't work for all grafts, especially the ones where the surrounding skin is relatively thin. In this case, I think we may be safe. If I can stretch the graft and stitch it into place and it holds, new skin, actually scar tissue, will grow into the gaps while it is healing. It might take a while, but it should work as long as the graft stays connected to the area."

"Really?" Captain Miller asked in surprise.

"Yes, sir. I am no plastic surgeon, and I have never tried anything like this before. Still, the technique is very straightforward, and even if it isn't completely successful, the patch should facilitate the healing process, and the Orca shouldn't be any worse off for trying it."

Captain Miller asked me, "Jack, do you think Jill can explain things to the Orcas?"

"Yes, sir, I have been relaying what Adrian has said. She already explained most of it in generalities. I have no idea what exactly she told them because she is in rapport at levels that are new to me. She's confident they understand or, more appropriately, that they trust us. How long do you think the preparation should take, Adrian?"

"Probably an hour or so," He replied.

"How can we help, Adrian?" Captain Miller asked.

"I'll need to use a sterile cutting board in the galley to do the trimming and preparation, if that would be okay, Captain."

Captain Miller turned to the Skipper of the Cutter, "Lieutenant?"

"Right this way, Doctor, I heard some pots rattling, so I think some of the crew have already started boiling water. Do you have scalpels, sir, or will you need us to hone and sterilize some of our galley knives?"

"I do have some scalpels, but I suspect they will dull fairly quickly because the skin is very tough. The boiling water will do to sterilize things. Not that they need to be particularly sterile considering the circumstances, but let's not take any chances." Adrian said as they followed Juanita Hernandez. Then he asked, "Do you have any alcohol that I can use to sterilize the cutting board?"

"Rubbing alcohol, will that do?"

"That would be perfect; thanks, Juanita."

While Adrian worked, Jill and Shirley continued to work with Sonny to keep him calm and relaxed, and the rest of us ate lunch. When he finished preparing the graft, Adrian and Chloe prepared hypodermics with the anesthetic and several suture kits with the strongest suture material. When the graft was ready, Adrian placed everything in the strongest plastic bags available. Then he asked, "Juanita, do you have a small life raft we can use to carry our stuff over to Sonny?"

"One of the things the Coast Guard is not short of, Adrian, is life rafts. Hang on a second; the locker is on the other side of the Cutter." Juanita cut through the command deck to the port side and returned a minute later with a small bundle. "Drop this in the water just before you go down the ladder. It is self-inflating, and there are several lines in the package for rigging a tow."

"Thanks, Juanita, okay folks, we had better get going before it gets much later," Adrian said as he once again pulled on Tom's wetsuit and then went down the side of the Cutter to the water. Chloe followed, wearing her T-shirt.

Once again, several Orcas swam over to tow the group into the cove. As advertised, the life raft inflated automatically, and the noise caused a momentary concern among the Orcas. But Jill explained things, and they calmed down.

As soon as they were on their way, Jill and Shirley went to work to calm Sonny for what was to come. Mother assured them that he was ready.

When Adrian and Chloe arrived, Chloe immediately began injecting the anesthetic into the area surrounding the wound, and Sonny never even flinched. Then Adrian, assisted by Chloe, stitched the patch into place. The process took over an hour, during which time Sonny remained calm and relaxed and held as still as possible. While Adrian was working, I informed everyone of the progress, as Jill relayed it to me. When they finished the graft, the Orcas returned all of them to the Cutter.

"How did it go?" Captain Miller asked as they were removing their wetsuits.

"Better than I expected," Adrian replied. "The patch covered about 85 percent of the wound area, and I don't think I could have stretched it any further without risking it tearing away. If he doesn't do anything to compromise the wound area, it should heal in a month or so. There will be scarring, of course, but we find scars of one sort or another on almost every whale or porpoise in the wild. In fact, one of the Orcas that towed us back to the Cutter had a chunk taken out of his dorsal fin, which seemed to have healed fine. Most are from shark bites or swimming too close to coral, or any of a dozen other causes, but they all heal given time."

"I'm amazed, Adrian. Simply amazed. Are we finished now?" Captain Miller asked. "I don't mean to rush you, but there has been a non-emergency call for the helicopter to return to its base."

"Yes, sir, we have done all that we can do. Now it is up to mother nature to finish the job."

While they were talking, Chloe changed back into the Coast Guard jumpsuit and prepared their equipment to leave. "I'll return the jumpsuit after I get home, Juanita." She said.

"Chloe, you may keep the jumpsuit as a memento of your visit with the Coast Guard." Lieutenant Hernandez said.

"Thank you, ma'am," Chloe said a big smile on her face.

"Thank you all," Captain Miller said, including everyone. "You all realize, of course, that nothing that happened here is to be reported to the media. As far as I am concerned, it is classified. That is why I sent Gunderson and Mortenstern to Port Angeles when I did so they could not see what was going on. I, for one, do not want to be accused of losing my mind, and we certainly do not want a media frenzy considering the effects it might have on the Orcas. If someone told me about the last two days, I would never believe him anyway, but some hotshot reporter could ruin it for all of us, especially the Orcas. You can count on me, the crew of the Cutter, and the helicopter as well, and I am sure Tom and Shirley will remain silent about what actually happened. As far as I am concerned, the

Orca strike was reported by an anonymous source, and we simply followed up the lead and found evidence corroborating the report.

"You have my word, Captain." I said.

"And ours, sir," Tom and Shirley nodded in agreement.

"As for you, Adrian and Chloe, I know the world of academia is different from ours, and something is bound to get out eventually. We will rely on your discretion for the moment. If you feel that you need to somehow publish what has happened, please obfuscate the report as much as possible."

"We will do that, sir, and I am sure Chloe agrees as well. Chloe?" Adrian asked.

"Oh, definitely, Captain, you can count on me." Chloe said in agreement.

"Good. Thanks to all of you for a fantastic experience." Captain Miller said. "Jack, the cutter crew will return you and Jill to your boat." He said to me.

Jill and I remained in the cove for more than an hour after the Coasties left before we said goodbye to the Orcas and left for home.

Two weeks later, we received a letter from Captain Miller containing a decal and pennant for our boat authorizing us to contact and observe Orcas in close proximity.

Several weeks passed before we were again trolling in the vicinity of what we now called 'Sonny's Island.' When we felt a gentle bump. When we looked over the side, it was Sonny who sky-scoped so Jill could touch him, and he squealed in a way that could only be interpreted as friendship and gratitude. Jill spoke with him briefly, and I heard him tell her his tail was okay now. Then he dove under the boat and breached to show us. When he breached, we could see the scar on his back, and it appeared to be healing well. While the rest of the pod was swimming nearby, Mother sky-scoped and also sent us a very strong feeling of gratitude before swimming away.

Since then, whenever we are in the vicinity of Sonny's Island and the pod is nearby, they swim by and actually greet us! It is always a thrill.

Part II

Mother's Tale

Sonny Seeks Help

Sam and Sylvia Worther were lying on the foredeck of their cabin cruiser drifting East along the Eastern end of the Strait of Juan de Fuca, soaking up the sunshine in the late afternoon. A light breeze out of the west kept them cool and drifting in the general direction of the Marina they had launched from at Everett. It had been a good day for fishing. The cooler contained a mixture of nice fat King and Silver salmon, enough to last them for a long time, and for a bonus, Sam had also caught a 35-pound Halibut off the entrance to Discovery Bay.

They had seen several Orcas while trolling and had lost one salmon when an Orca took it right off the hook close to the boat as they were reeling it in. However, that was common enough that none of the fishermen minded losing one once in a while for an opportunity to see an Orca up close.

"Well, babe, have you had enough sunshine for one day?" Sam asked his wife.

"Yup. anymore, and I might burn. I wish I had your complexion, so I didn't have to worry about burning." Sylvia replied as she sat up and began to roll up the beach towels they had been lying on.

As she started back to the cockpit, an Orca came up about 20 feet from the side of the boat and sky-scoped while chattering Orca sounds. It then slipped back underwater and came up a little further away while doing the same thing. It seemed like it was trying to tell them something. It did this several times, and then it seemed to leave. When the Orca left, they hurried back to the cockpit.

"What do you think about that, Syl?" Sam asked.

"Strange. But considering the new distancing rules, we had better call the Washington Fish and Wildlife office and report it before somebody else tells them what happened and tries to blame it on us. What do you think?"

"I agree. Where is the rule book? I think the phone number is on it." he replied.

Sylvia rummaged through the glove compartment, found the WDFW rule book, and handed it to Sam, who had his cell phone in hand. He keyed in the phone number and waited while it rang.

"WDFW, my name is Dave Smith." A man answered, "How can I help you?".

"We need to report an Orca encounter out in the Strait, Mr. Smith," Sam said.

"How close?" the man asked.

"Twenty to thirty feet."

"Did you touch it?"

"Good lord, no!" Sam exclaimed. "But it was well within the 500-yard distance rule."

"Okay," the man said. "I'm going to transfer you to Shirley White in the Aquatic Mammals Section. Hang on."

"Thanks, Dave," Sam replied.

A moment later, a woman's voice said. "Aquatic Mammals, Cetaceous Unit, Shirley White speaking, how can I help you?"

"My name is Sam Worther, and my wife Sylvia and I would like to report an Orca encounter a while ago at the east end of the Strait. I'm calling because it was very close to our boat and well within the new 500-yard limit." Sam said.

"Okay, My Worther, tell me what happened," Shirley asked.

"Well, we were drifting while catching some rays on the front deck of our boat when this Orca reared up out of the water alongside us and made a lot of strange sounds, sort of a chattering, if you know what I mean," Sam replied.

"How close?" She asked.

"Fifteen feet or so at the beginning and then a little farther out, maybe thirty or forty feet a couple of times, then it swam away." He replied.

"Did you pursue it?" She asked.

"Absolutely not!" Sam exclaimed defensively.

"Can you describe the animal, Sam?" Shirley asked.

"What do you mean? An Orca is an Orca. isn't it?" He said.

"Not necessarily. For instance, do you think it was a male or a female?" Shirley asked.

"Are you serious, Ms. White? How the hell could I possibly know that?" Sam replied.

"It's not as difficult as you might think. For instance, could you see the dorsal fin?" Shirley clarified.

"The one on it's back, you mean?" Sam asked.

"Yes, was it tall or short? Male Orcas have tall dorsal fins, and females have a shorter fin that even sags a little sometimes." Shirley said.

"I guess you would call it tall, and it looked like it stood straight up. Why all the questions? Am I in some kind of trouble?" Sam asked, clearly concerned.

"Relax, Sam. I assure you that you are not in any trouble." Shirley tried to assure him. "Quite the contrary, you have been a big help."

"Really?" He asked, somewhat surprised.

"Yes, really. I got a call just before you called from an observer on a nearby island who reported the encounter and described what happened exactly like you did."

"Good grief, would I have been in trouble if I hadn't called you?" Sam asked.

"No, you could not have avoided the encounter. That Orca has been doing this for the past few days, and you are the only one who called it in. Sam, could you please describe your boat?" she asked.

"It's a pretty common inboard older wooden cabin cruiser. It is about twenty-three feet long."

"What color is it?" Shirley asked.

"The hull is painted white, and the cabin, cockpit, and deck are mahogany varnished natural wood color. Is that what you mean?"

"Yes, that's a perfect description. But, believe it or not, you just told me why the Orca came to your boat." Shirley said, then followed with, "About two years ago, a couple with a boat very similar to yours helped an Orca in distress. Did you notice any markings on him, like color patches, for instance?"

"I don't know, let me think, and I'll ask my wife. Honey, did you see any markings on the Orca?"

"I don't think so, Sam. It had the usual color patch behind its fin. Oh, and I did see a white spot about the size of a coffee saucer on its back just ahead of its tail." Sylvia replied. "Is that what she means?"

"Could you hear her, Shirley?" Sam asked.

"Yes!" Shirley replied vehemently, "Yes. that is a perfect description of a youngish male orca we have named Sonny. He was involved in an encounter with a fishing boat a couple of years ago that left him with a white scar on his back near his flukes. Thank you very much, Sam and Sylvia. You have cleared up a mystery. Thanks again for calling us. We truly appreciate it."

"You're most welcome, Shirley. Goodbye." Sam said.

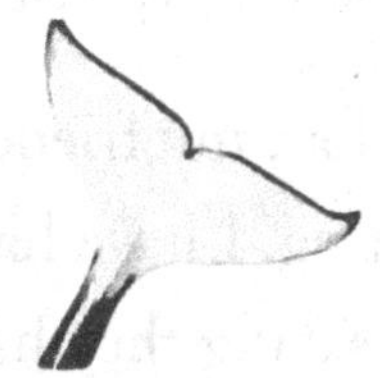

WDFW Takes a Hand

The words on the frosted glass panel of the office door said,

Washington State Department
Fish and Wildlife
Salt Water Mammals Division
Supervisory Game Warden
Thomas Broderick

Shirley White, Cetaceous Unit Director, hesitated outside Broderick's office before rapping on the glass panel, then knocked.

"Enter," came a man's voice from within.

Shirley opened the door and walked into the office, and said, "Hi, Tom. Are you busy?"

"Never too busy for you. I've been trying to find something significant to say in the quarterly report. Unfortunately, things have been kind of dull around here since last quarter's report."

"Well, hang onto your hat, my friend, because things are about to get much more interesting. I have had five telephone calls from whale watchers this week saying they have seen an Orca appearing to harass boaters."

"Have the boaters been within the 500-yard distance order," Tom asked.

"Yes, and some have been very close," she replied.

"Did they get the boater's identification?" he asked.

"Yes, they reported the boater's identification on three of the incidents and just the boat size and colors on the others. But, here is the rub. It was not the boaters' fault. They were all in clear water, nowhere near any Orca pods. Instead, the Orca approached the boats and sky scoped with its head out of the water and then dove and swam away from the boats."

"What!" Tom exclaimed, surprised. "That's a new one on me."

"Oh, it gets better. I just had a telephone call from one of the boaters who described their encounter in detail. Tom, it's Sonny who is approaching the boats looking for something and, not finding it, swims away. This man said that Sonny swam up to just 15 to 20 feet away and chattered and clicked at them for a while before he swam away. I know it is Sonny because this man, or more specifically his wife, described the patch on the Orca's back near the tail perfectly."

"I'll be damned," Tom exclaimed. Why this boat?"

"I wondered that too, so I asked him to describe his boat, and the description matches the description of the Kline's cabin cruiser to a tee."

"Do you think he is looking for the Klines?" Tom asked.

"Yes, I do. He wants something he thinks they can do." she answered.

"Where did this incident occur?" Tom asked.

"Not just this incident, according to the watchers, they all occurred near the east end of the Strait of Juan de Fuca in the pass between Port Townsend and Whidbey Island, actually between Marrowstone Island and Whidbey Island. That's where the salmon are running best at this time."

"What do you suppose he wants?" Tom asked.

"I have no idea, but I'll bet I can find someone who can find out what he wants?" Shirley replied.

"The Klines?" Tom asked.

"Yup, if anybody can figure out what is going on, especially if Mother is around, they can," Shirley replied.

"Well, I suppose you ought to call the Klines and see if they want to get involved. Do you have their telephone number handy?" Tom asked.

"Yes, sir. I hoped you might suggest that." Shirley replied. "It's right here in my cell phone."

"Great, call from here, why don't you? I suppose we should both be in on the call." Tom said.

The Klines Are Called

It was a warm spring Sunday morning. Jack Kline was lying on a recliner on the patio under the comic section of the Seattle Times, which was providing shade from the sun while he snoozed when his cell phone rang,

Jill, his wife, who was planting some flowers near the back of the property, called out, "Can you get the phone, Honey?"

"Got it," He replied, casting aside the paper and picking up his cell phone from the table beside the recliner.

He looked at the screen. He saw the Washington State Department of Fish and Wildlife in big, bold letters. That got his instant attention because he had worked with the WDFW a few years before.

"Hello, Jack Kline speaking, what can I do you for?" He asked.

"Hi, Jack. This is Shirley White with Tom Broderick. We met a couple of years ago up in the Strait when you and Jill were helping a wounded juvenile Orca."

"Who is it?" Jill asked as she approached the patio.

"Hang on, Shirley. Jill is coming." He replied to Shirley. Then to Jill, "It's Shirley White from the WDFW, Honey."

"What does she want?" Jill asked.

"I don't know, I just picked up the phone," he said.

"Hi, Shirley, how goes it," Jill said, looking over Jack's shoulder.

Then Jack asked, "What can we do for you, Shirley?"

"Guys, we have a problem," Shirley said. "We have had several calls from Orca observers and one from a fisherman complaining that an Orca is bothering the fishermen out in the Strait by coming up near their boats, sky scoping and clicking and squealing. The Orca seems to wait by their boats for a few minutes, then disappears. From the description given by the fisherman who called today, I think it is probably Sonny. He said the Orca swam right up to their boat then they saw a small white patch on the back near its tail as it swam away. I asked him to describe his boat, and it sounded very similar to yours."

"Oh, my God!" Jill exclaimed.

"Do you still have your boat?" Shirley asked.

"Oh, yeah, we still have it," Jack replied. "Jill has been having some health problems, so we haven't been fishing so far this year."

"Can you come now?" Tom interjected.

"Yes," they replied in chorus. "Give us a day to get everything together, hook up the boat, and we can be on our way. Where do you want us to go to?"

"There is a marina in Everett which is near where the incidents have occurred," Tom said.

"Okay, I know where it is. We will be there tomorrow before noon. Can you call the Marina and let them know we are coming?" Jack asked.

"I'll do that," Shirley replied, "and text you the address, etcetera, and I will be there to meet you, and let's have lunch in the restaurant when you arrive, okay? Oh, I almost forgot. Tom said WDFW would foot the costs, including mileage. Can I come with you in your boat?"

"Great, we will look forward to seeing you, and you are always welcome to join us in our boat," Jack replied.

"We'd better get going if we are going to get there tomorrow," Jill said. "I'll pack our stuff while you get the boat in shape to tow, Okay?"

"Yes, dear!" Jack replied with false emphasis as he headed towards the garage to prepare for the outing. "I'll need to go and get air for the dive tanks and gas for the boat and car, so I will be gone a while. When I get home, do you have any thoughts on what I should do with the stuff that has been piling up in the boat for the past two years?"

"Thank you, darling. I wondered about that myself." Jill answered. "I guess you or we will just have to pile it in the corner for the time being. Okay?"

"Okay," Jack replied.

"Do you think you will be home for dinner?" Jill asked. Then laughed as she headed for the bedroom to pack the clothes they might need.

"I'll be home for dinner," Jack answered from the garage as he piled the last of the things that had accumulated in the boat on the garage floor. He then closed the door to the house, hooked up the boat to the car, and drove off to the dive shop and gas station.

Two hours later, he parked in front of the house and, whistling a tuneless ditty sauntered up the walk into the garage and through the door into the house, announcing himself home for dinner. "Hi, Jill, what's cookin', good lookin'?" he said as he kissed her on the back of the neck.

"Kielbasa and kraut, as if you couldn't smell it." She responded over her shoulder, sniffed, then added, "Phew, what have you been drinking?"

"Dave, over to the dive shop, is celebrating his tenth year in business with a jug of something sent to him by his father from Eastern Europe. A bunch of guys were there. We had a congratulations party." He replied, slightly slurring his words.

"Hmm, will you be okay to drive in the morning?" Jill asked.

"Yes, I will," he responded clearly, "I only had two small glasses. Ugh, what awful stuff it was. I'll wash up and join you at the table in five minutes, okay?"

"Okay!"

"Okay."

In the morning, right after breakfast, the Klines pulled away from their home south of Seattle and headed for Everett to meet up with Shirley. As they turned onto I-5 North south of Olympia, Jill asked, "What are you thinking would be the best route, Jack?"

"Yeah, I've been wondering about that too. We could stay on I-5 up through Seattle, but this is a weekday and I-5 through Seattle is awful on weekdays especially hauling a boat. We could do the freeway runaround, but that is further and not much better. So what do you say to going up I-5 through Tacoma and across the Takoma Narrows Bridge to WA 16 and 3 up to Kingston to take the Kingston-Edmond Ferry and then up to the Everett Marina from there and bypass Seattle altogether, Hon?"

"I like it. It's a nice drive, and it should be wide open most of the way and, in the end, faster, even allowing for the ferry." Jill replied.

"Great," Jack said.

Rescue Team in Everett

Three and a half hours later, as they turned into the entrance to the Everett Marina, they were greeted by Shirley who was sitting on the fence and waving. "Hi, guys. The Marina is expecting you, and the state is paying the bill, follow me, and we will get you launched." She led them down to the boat ramp, and 10 minutes later, the boat was in the water, tied to the dock. Are you ready for lunch?"

"We are," Jill replied. "Lead on."

After ordering lunch and sitting sipping their coffee, Shirley observed, "I see you two are wearing beachwear, and I have my swimsuit on under my uniform, so I guess we are ready to go after we eat."

"We figured it would be faster this way, and changing in the cabin on the boat can literally be a pain," Jill said.

"Oh, I meant to tell you. You'll never guess what happened when I got here and walked out on the dock. Sonny was about twenty yards away in the Strait, and I think he saw me and recognized me. Because, he came right up to the dock and chittered at me while sky-scoping. Everybody at the Marina saw him and came running. But he swam away before more than a couple of people got too close. And, if you will give it a gander, there he is now, looking for us." She said as she pointed out into the entrance to the Marina.

Jack and Jill looked where Shirley was pointing and saw Sonny as he sky-scoped and chittered again.

"Hi." A man's voice said as he walked up to their table. "Are you Shirley White, perchance?"

"I sure am," Shirley replied, smiling. "Who's asking?"

"I'm Sam Worther with my wife, Sylvia." The voice replied. "I saw your uniform and wondered if you were here about that Orca out there. He looks like the one I called you about who approached our boat the other day."

"Hi Sam, pleased to meet you both," Shirley replied, then added. "This is Jack and Jill Kline, and it is their boat you saw. They are the folks I told you about who helped the Orcas a couple of years ago."

"Pleased to meet you both," Sam said. "I heard rumors about what happened and was surprised when he came up very close to us the other day. Then I saw your boat when you drove into the Marina, and the bell rang. Your boat and ours are almost identical. Are you here to work with him again? Sorry, that was a dumb question. Of course, you are."

"Actually, we are not too sure just why we are here. From the way he is acting out in the strait, he looks like he is okay, but he must have some reason, something is on his mind, or he would not have contacted you." Jack explained.

"I thought as much and hoped we could join you if you are going to help again," Sam said, raising an eyebrow to punctuate the question.

Shirley paused, then turned to Jack and said, "It's up to you, Jack. It's your boat."

Jack thought for a moment, then replied, "Like you, we only have four seats, so it'll be a bit crowded if you don't mind."

"I'll sit on the cooler." Shirley offered.

Then, Sam interjected. "Nope, why don't you and Sylvia sit in the back seats, and I will sit on the cooler if that is okay with everyone? We'll do our best to keep out of the way and help wherever and whenever we can." Sam added.

"Right!" Jack said as he led the way to the boat where he helped Sylvia step down into the cockpit and guided her to the portside rear seat. Then he helped Shirley to sit on the starboard side seat, leaving Sam to find his way to the cooler.

As Sam stepped down into the cockpit, Jill stood up and stepped away from her usual copilot seat and said, "Sam, why don't you sit up here with Jack, and I'll sit on the cooler back with Sylvia and Shirley?"

Sam started to object, and Jill interrupted with, "Please, I insist." Sam nodded politely and took the indicated seat.

"Is everyone comfortable?" Jack asked in jest as he started the engine and turned the boat towards where Sonny was sky-scoping.

Then Sonny swam up to the side of the boat, bumped it gently, and swam out into the Strait and sky-scoped again.

"Now, that was a let's get going if I ever saw one," Shirley said.

Everyone laughed, and Jack steered the boat out towards Sonny.

Sonny immediately began to swim north up the channel. A mile and a half later, he stopped near what appeared to be a shallow area where the state had a preserve set aside for a Sea Weed and Kelp Forest and salmon habitat.

[Help, we]. Jill gasped in surprise. "I just heard Mother ask for help. It was clear but weak. Jack, it's Mother and she must be nearby." Jill said. "She's calling for help and her call seems to be much weaker than it has ever been before. How deep is the water here?"

"It depends on just where," Jack replied. "According to the Fathometer, it varies from 20 to 40 feet. Right here, it is about 32 feet, but where is she?"

Sam turned around to look at Jill, "You heard what?" he asked, bewildered.

"I'll explain," Shirley offered and continued. "If that is okay with you, Jill."

"Please do," Jill answered. "I'll go down in the cabin and get out of my duds and into my wet suit. Meanwhile, Jack, please get my scuba gear ready, just in case."

"Will do, and Sam, would you please drop the anchor and let out about 15 feet of line to swing," Jack asked.

"Sure thing," Sam replied and did as asked. Then he turned to Shirley and said, "You were going to explain what has happened?"

Before Shirley could answer, Jill came back on deck and said. "I suspect that if she were capable, she would have come up to the surface when we got close, wouldn't she? So my guess is that one of us will have to dive down to find her. I can free-dive down sixteen to twenty feet, so I will take a pair of goggles and have a look."

"Okay, Hon, I'll be watching you on the Fathometer. But I suggest you follow the anchor line in case we need to pull you up."

"Good idea, I'll do just that." As she said that, Jill took several deep breaths, lowered herself over the side of the boat, and dove down following the anchor line. As she dove, she looked all around the area for Mother.

Once Jill began her dive Shirley told Sam and Sylvia about Jack and Jill. "Jack and Jill are mutually telepathic. They can communicate without using words. Two years ago, Mother, as they call her, connected with them out in the Strait after Sonny was deliberately injured by a speeding fishing boat. What followed was nearly unbelievable. The short version is that they, Jack and Jill, coordinated the treatment of the young Orca by assisting a Veterinary team from the University of Oregon in treating the injured Orca by acting as a communication link between the Vets and the Orca pod leader whom they dubbed Mother. The Coast Guard was involved and completely supported the whole process. That is why that Orca contact flag is on the mast and decals on both sides of the boat."

"[I see you, do you see her?]" Jack asked. Then added, "[Okay, but don't stay down too long. You know your lungs aren't as good as they were.]"

Shirley continued her explanation, "He will speak aloud what he is getting from her and what he says to her so that we can be part of the conversation and not be left in the dark."

"Well, I'll be damned," Sam exclaimed.

"Me too," Sylvia added with a smile.

"[Okay, Jill come on back up.]" He turned to Sam, "Watch for her as she comes up, and if she has a problem, haul her in."

"Yes, sir," Sam replied, keeping a firm grip on the anchor line. When Jill surfaced, Sam helped her back into the boat. Sylvia wrapped her in a big beach towel to dry her and help her keep warm.

"The visibility is not as good as I had hoped," Jill explained. "I could see some of the bottom, but it is not uniform, so some of it is out of view. I could sense that she was not far off, but I couldn't see her. I guess I'll need to use the Scuba gear to do a better search. I think it would be handy if we wrapped a tether around the anchor line to keep me connected but still give me some room to maneuver."

"Sam?" Jack asked.

"On it," Sam said as he tied a ring to the top of the line he used as the tether and tied a mechanical clip to the end of the line, wrapped the line around the anchor line, and clipped it to the ring. "Do you think there is anything else we can do to make it easier, Jack? How about pulling up the anchor line so she can use the anchor's weight to haul her down."

"Not off hand, a lot will depend on what she sees down there, and we need the anchor to keep us in position now and while she is down there," Jack said.

"Yes, of course," Sam said.

"Okay, I'm ready," Jill said as she sat on the gunnel and did the back flop into the water. Sam held the tether so it wouldn't get tangled, then let go. "G'bye guys, be back soon."

As soon as Jill went under Jack asked, "[Is everything okay?]" and nodded saying, "[so far so good.]"

Shirley explained, "As I said before, when Jack talks to her telepathically in the presence of others, he always says what he said to her out loud so everyone can hear, and he says out loud whatever she replies. There will be chit-chat between them which he might not say aloud. But, if it is important, you will know it."

"Amazing," Sam exclaimed. "I wouldn't believe it if I hadn't seen it with my own eyes and heard it with my own ears. How about you, Sylvia?"

"I'll second that!" Sylvia replied.

"[Okay, pull me up, please.]"

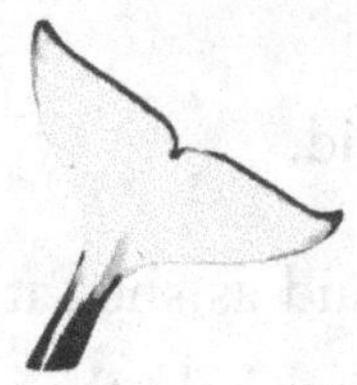

Mother being Attacked

As Sam was reeling Jill in hand over hand, something caught his eye. "Hey, guys, can you see what those kids are doing over there on the beach?"

Shirley stepped up on the rear seat with a pair of binoculars and focused them on the beach and the children. "They're throwing rocks at something right over there." She said, pointing at something in the water near the shore. "It looks a little like a log or clump of seaweed."

As Jill rose to the surface, Jack asked. "[She's what?]" Before Jill could answer, she surfaced next to the boat. "Something or somebody is hurting Mother! She says."

"Shirley, please hand me the binoculars." Sam said as he stepped up onto the rear seat next to her.". He focused them on the object on the beach and said. "Son of a bitch, they are throwing rocks and sticks at an Orca which is in the surf in shallow water near the beach, and the parents are there encouraging them."

"Get the anchor up, please, Sam," Shirley said. "And, Jack, as soon as it is clear of the bottom, start the engine and head for the beach over there. They are throwing stones at Mother."

Jack reached over the side of the boat and helped Sam lift Jill into the boat, then started the engine. "Are you sure it's okay to go through the kelp forest, Shirley?" Jack asked.

"Anchor is up, Jack," Sam said.

"Hell yes," Shirley replied. "I am a game warden and a State Official. I'll take responsibility if it comes to that. Head right for those kids that are throwing the rocks."

As soon as Jack began to head for the beach, the parents called the children and started to leave.

Shirley picked up the bullhorn she carried onto the boat just in case, and said. "Stop where you are! I am an official of the Washington Division of Fish and Wildlife, and you are under arrest for molesting and injuring wildlife."

"Bull shit!" the father exclaimed. "It's a dead Orca!"

"No, sir, she is an injured Orca needing help. She is not dead." Shirley retorted as Jack ran the boat up onto the beach near where the people had stopped. Shirley jumped over the side and waded ashore, showing the uniform and badge.

"It looks like it is dead!" the man explained, "the kids were just having some fun."

"You call torturing and molesting an injured animal fun?" Shirley retorted.

"It is not moving, is it?" The man asked.

"Look carefully, sir, and you will see that it rises to breathe and exhales. Now, I will need to see your driver's license and your hunting license."

The husband pulled out his wallet and removed his driver's license. "I have a fishing license, but I don't have a hunting license. Will that do?"

"I'll see." She said as she inspected the licenses. "Well, Mr. Wilkerson, after all, a fishing license is not a license to hunt or kill aquatic mammals, is it?"

While Shirley was dealing with the family, the rest of the boat's occupants had waded ashore and headed for Mother.

Mother sees Jill

When Mother saw Jill she began squealing and clicking and moving a little.

"She recognizes me," Jill said as she waded into the surf to where Mother was and stroked her.

"Can I touch her?" Sylvia asked as she waded into the surf towards Shirley and Mother.

"Yes, let me introduce you first. Give me your hand." Jill replied, then took Sylvia's hand, led her around to where Mother could see her, then she took Sylvia's hand and placed it on Mother's nose where she could see it, and said, "[new friend.]"

Mother clicked in response and lifted her head a little nudging Sylvia.

Sylvia burst into tears as she stroked Mother gently.

"That gives me an idea," Jill exclaimed. "Shirley, why don't you bring the family over here to see Mother up close."

"Great idea, Jill." Shirley replied and then walked over to the family and said, "Come with me, please, and see the animal you were throwing rocks at."

"Is it safe? For the kids, I mean." Mr. Wilkerson said. "After all, she is a killer whale, isn't she?"

"It's unusual, but I know her," Shirley answered. "Also, you should know that with one exception, no Orca has ever injured a human being, and there are a good many examples of where they actually helped people. Follow me, please, all of you."

Mother meets family

As they were walking toward where Jill and Sylvia were standing with Mother, Sylvia was blotting her tears. Then she said, "I petted her, and she seemed to thank me. She is completely safe, but I suggest you go to her one at a time."

Shirley led the family over to the beach near Mother. Then said, "See the lady in the wet suit? She can talk to the Orca, whom we know as 'Mother' because she is the mother of the pod. I will take you one at a time out in the water to see her up close. If you are very careful, you may gently touch or pet her on her nose. She is in a great deal of pain, and as you can see from the look of her skin, she is ill and starving."

"Is she ready, Jill?" Shirley asked.

Jill looked at Mother and said, "[May they touch you if they are careful?]"

"[Yes]" Mother replied.

Shirley said, "Thanks, Sylvia," then she looked at the family, thought for a moment, then said, "Who wants to be first?"

"Me, Daddy, please." The young daughter asked her Father and turned to Shirley, "Me please, Miss White?"

"Your name, dear?" Shirley asked.

"Becky." The girl replied.

"Mr. Wilkerson?" Shirley asked.

Wilkerson looked dubious and saw Sylvia nod, then he shrugged his shoulders and said, "Go ahead, Becky, but be very careful."

"I will, Daddy, I promise," Becky said and went over to where Shirley was waiting for her.

"Give me your hand, Becky, and come with me," Shirley said as she offered her hand.

They walked hand in hand out into the surf where Jill was with Mother, and Shirley handed the girl over to Jill, who took Becky's hand and placed it on Mother's nose while saying, aloud and telepathically to Mother, [new friend] and surprisingly Becky said "new friend" too.

Mother lifted her head a little and clicked. Becky bent down and petted Mother as her parents gasped. Then Becky got up and ran back to her family, saying, "Mother, I did it, I touched the Orca, and she touched me back."

Mrs. Wilkerson was standing dumbfounded with tears running down her face as she held her daughter and said, "I am so proud of you, Becky."

"Would any other of you wish to come and meet the Orca?" Shirley asked.

Mr. Wilkerson and his son both shook their heads no. But Mrs. Wilkerson walked over to Shirley and said, "Miss White, may I meet the Orca, please?"

"Sure, Mrs. Wilkerson, my name is Shirley, and yes, you may. Please come with me," Shirley said as she led the woman over to Jill.

"Jill, this is," Shirley began.

"Daisy," Mrs. Wilkerson said, "Pleased to meet you and thank you for what you have done for our family. Now, may I pet or touch her as well, please?"

Jill took Daisy's hand and, as with Becky, placed it on Mother's nose, saying, "[New friend]" aloud and telepathically to Mother.

Daisy said, "Pleased to meet you, Mother is it?"

Mother gave a slight shake and some clicking which Jill said as "[good]".

When Daisy stood up, she said, "Shirley and Jill, if there is anything we can do to help, just ask. It may not be much, but I, for one, and Becky too, have been touched by what has happened here. How long do you think you will be working here?"

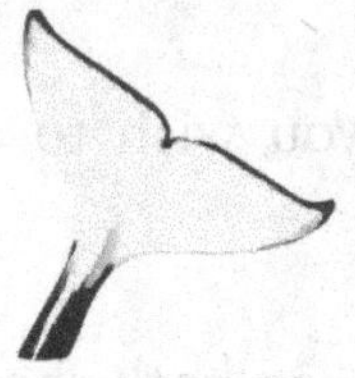

Rescue Begins

"We just got started," Shirley replied. "We are going to try to rescue Mother, and considering her condition, that may take quite a while if it is even possible."

"Would it be okay if we came by from time to time and offered what help we can give?" Daisy asked.

"Yes, feel free to do that, but keep it under your hat because we do not need to be inundated with "Lookie Lous" treading around and disrupting our work so they can say they saw a dying Orca and take pictures."

"I promise. It may be hard to keep the kids quiet about it, especially Becky, but I don't think she knows exactly where we are, so there should not be any risk of exposure."

After the Wilkersons left, Jill asked, "Shirley, what do we do now? Do you suppose we can call for Adrian to come up here again like last time?"

"I was wondering the same thing." Shirley replied, "I'll call Tom and see what he can do, okay?" Then she took out her cell phone and placed the call.

"Washington State Department of Fish and Wildlife, Salt Water Mammals Division, Supervisory Game Warden Thomas Broderick's Office. This is Maureen Carter speaking. How may I help you?"

"Hi, Maureen," Shirley replied. "This is Shirley. Is Tom in?"

"Oh, hi, Shirley. Yes, he is in, hang on." Maureen replied.

Shirley could hear her paging Tom, who picked up the phone immediately.

"Hi, Shirley. What's up with the Orcas?" Tom asked.

"We have a serious problem here, Tom. Mother, you remember the Orca we called Mother, don't you? Anyway, Mother is up near Everett in the surf of the Kelp Forest reserve, and she is in real distress."

"What is the matter with her?" Tom asked.

"We are not sure what is wrong, but it looks as if she is starving. Her coat is dingy and wrinkled, and she is in obvious distress. Do you think we could get your brother-in-law to come up and see what he could do to help her?" Shirley replied.

"He left Oregon and went down to head the department at one of the Universities in the Los Angeles area last year. I don't remember which one, but I can call down to Oregon and see who is there and whether they can tell me where he went. So, I'll give it a try and call you back." Tom said.

"Okay, I will stand by here." Then added as she saw the Klines signaling their greetings. "Oh, Tom, Jack, and Jill are here and waving hello."

"Hi, folks," Tom said. "I'm glad you could make it. Do you have any ideas what might be wrong with the Orca?"

"She's definitely ill, Tom," Shirley replied. "She looks horrible, all wrinkly and almost puffing or gasping to breathe. And she could get sunburn if she stays out in the daylight very long. I think we should probably cover her with a beach blanket and sprinkle water on it to keep her wet and cool."

"Sounds like a good idea. I will get back to you as soon as I can get in contact with the Oregon Institute of Marine Studies to see what they suggest." Tom Replied.

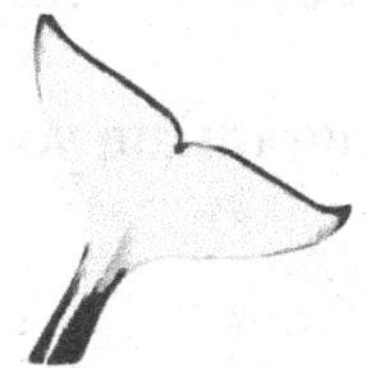

Calling for Help

"Oregon Institute of Marine Studies, How may I direct your call?" The operator announced.

"This is Thomas Broderick of The Washington State Department of Fish and Wildlife, Salt Water Mammals Division, and I would like to speak to Dr. Adrian Goodhurst or his replacement. Please, this is urgent."

"Yes, sir, I remember you from Dr. Goodhurst's going away party. I can connect you with Dr. Chloe Archer. She has been the acting Director since Dr. Goodhurst left a couple of months ago."

"That would be great. I know Dr. Archer." Tom said.

"Just a moment, sir. Dr. Archer is on the line Mr. Broderick." The operator finished.

"Hello, Tom," Chloe said warmly. "I haven't heard from you in, is it, a couple of years. Sorry I missed you at Adrian's party, but I had other commitments. What can I do for you?"

"First, Dr. Archer, I congratulate you on your new position. Is it permanent?"

"It's temporary at the moment. Adrian recommended me, but I don't have as much experience as the Institute would prefer. But they haven't had much success finding someone else either. So, for the time being, I am it. What can I do for you?"

"Remember Mother from when you were here with Adrian a couple of years ago?"

"I sure do. Is there a problem there?" Chloe asked.

"Yeah, it would seem that she is in distress and has beached herself or almost beached herself in the surf near Everett, Washington. From what Shirley, you remember Shirley, don't you, has told me, Mother is probably dying of starvation for some reason, but she is alert and able to communicate with Jill Kline."

"Sure, I remember Shirley and Jack and Jill Kline and just about everybody else who was there. If you noticed, my last name is no longer Crocker. I married Bobby Archer, one of the helicopter pilots who brought us up there two years ago. Anyway, what can I do to help?"

"Is there any possibility that you could come up here and help us out with Mother? She is in pretty bad shape and needs help as soon as possible. She is submerged in very shallow water with only her blow hole above the surface. They have covered her with a beach blanket and are doing everything to keep her covered and wet to prevent sunburn, according to Shirley."

"That is certainly the correct thing to do. You might commend them for that. Now, let me see what I can do. I have your number. I'll call you right back, okay Tom?"

"Okay, I'll be standing by, right here, goodbye."

Chloe used her cell phone to call her husband at work.

Bobby Archer answered the call, almost immediately, "Hi, Honey, what's up?"

"Bobby, remember when we met up in Washington when you flew Adrian and me up to the Strait to work on the injured Orca?"

Coast Guard to help

"Of course, now what?" he replied.

"I just got a call from Tom Broderick. You met him there. He is the director of the Washington Division of Fish and Wildlife Salt Water Mammals Division, and they have another problem with a sick or injured Orca. In this case, it is the mother of the one we cared for before, and she is in really bad shape. According to Tom, she is dying of possible starvation or injury and has almost beached herself because she is so weak. Tom has asked if I can come up and help, but it might take too long for me to drive. Do you think you could fly me up there ASAP, please?"

"Just a minute, hang on a minute. I'm having a late lunch with my Commander, and he has heard our conversation." Bobby said, then turning to the base Commander asked, "What about it, Commander Davis, could we do that?"

Commander Davis turned to the helicopter crew chief, "What about it, Chief, are both choppers in full working order? We might need one in case of an emergency here."

"They are both in A-1 condition Skipper so we could spare one of them for a couple of days. If we needed the second one, they would only be about three hours away, sir." The Crew Chief replied.

"Thanks, Chief. Tell her okay, Lieutenant. When you go, why don't you take Lieutenant Simms with you so he can get some stick time in traffic." The Commander said.

"Yes, sir, and I would be happy to take Tim along." Then to his phone, "Did you hear that, Chloe? I think we could pick you up on the school helipad in about 45 minutes."

"Great, I'll be ready, and I would like to bring my assistant if that would be okay?" Chloe asked.

"No problem with the assistant, Honey. See you in a bit." Bobby said.

"Excuse me, Lieutenant," Commander Davis interjected, "Wasn't Captain Miller from Port Angeles involved last time?"

"Yes, sir, he was. Are you thinking of coming along this time, Skipper?"

"Sure, why not? The more, the merrier. Chief, wind number 7 up if you please. I'll get my go-bag and meet you at the helipad in ten."

"Did you hear that, Honey? The cavalry is on its way. See you shortly." Bobby said.

"Sounds like a party from here. We will be on the helipad and awaiting your arrival. See you then." Chloe replied and hung up.

Forty-five minutes later, Chloe and her assistant Janice Williams were at the Institute's helipad watching the helicopter approaching for landing. As soon as it was down, they rushed out and got aboard.

"Hi, Sweetheart, and, oh, hi, Commander Davis, you came too, good," Chloe said.

"Yup, I couldn't let Captain Miller have all the fun, could I?" the Commander replied.

As soon as they were seated and belted in, Lieutenant Archer lifted the helicopter off and asked, "Where are we going, honey? We need to file a flight plan and get routing around Seattle."

"According to Shirley, they are north of Seattle and north of Everett and the Everett marina at a kelp forest reserve. They are going to get the employee's parking lot at the Marina cleared for you. Does that answer your question, Commander?"

"Yes, Dr. Archer, I think that will do nicely. However, did you happen to notice which helicopter we brought?" Commander Davis asked.

"No sir, what is different about this helicopter, sir?" Chloe replied, then she looked out to see what he was hinting about. "Okay, Commander, what is special about this helicopter?"

"Look at the landing gear, Dr. Archer." He said with a smirky smile.

She looked again and exclaimed, "Oh, my God, I didn't see that when we boarded. It looked just like a slightly higher step." Then she turned to her assistant, pointed, and said, Janice, this copter has pontoons. We don't need to land anywhere except near the beach.

I'm going to call Shirley and let her know that we don't need a parking lot."

Chloe called Shirley White on her cell phone.

Shirley picked up her phone and, noting who was calling, answered, "Hi Chloe, what's up?"

"We are on our way, Shirley. The Coast Guard is bringing us, and we are on a helicopter with pontoon landing gear so we can land right where you are."

"That's great! It makes things much easier all around. See you soon."

Commander Davis clicked the intercom to get the pilot's attention, then said, "Lieutenant, let's fly low up the west side of the Sound past Seatac Airport and Everett Field air traffic and wrap around south of Whidbey Island to find where they are. The Marina is not on this chart, but it shouldn't be too hard to find. I'll clear us with Seattle area traffic control and tell them our destination."

"Roger," Lieutenant Archer replied and edged over to the west side of Puget Sound.

Forty minutes later, they had passed the Seattle and Everett airport approaches and turned into Possession Sound, headed towards Priest Point and Mission Beach.

Suddenly Chloe pointed toward the beach and said, "There they are over there to the right. See them waving?."

"Got it," Bobby said, then added, "I think we should go on past them and swing around pointing south so we can land into the wind nearest the beach right in front of their boat so we don't blow sand and stuff on them."

Coast Guard Arrives

"Sounds good to me," Commander Davis replied.

"We will need an anchor or tiedown to keep from drifting if we land on the water, sir." Tim commented, then added, "Do you think the beach is flat enough to land on it?"

"It looks okay to me," Commander Davis said as he pointed at what appeared to be a reasonably flat area near where the people on the beach were standing. "Archer, let's land pointing inland, and we will be nose high. There is a slight crosswind from the south, but I don't think that should be a problem."

"Yes, sir." Bobby Archer replied as he waved at the people on the beach and pointed toward where he intended to land.

On the beach, Shirley and Jill waved at Chloe, who was waving out the helicopter window. As soon as the rotor stopped turning, they ran to the helicopter and hugged Chloe as she stepped onto the beach.

"Hi, guys. Happy to see you," Chloe said, smiling. "It's been a long time, hasn't it? First, let me introduce everyone. "Shirley White," she said, indicating Shirley, "and Jill Kline and her husband, Jack. Friends, this is my husband, Bobby Archer, and his commanding officer Commander Richard Davis and our copilot Ensign Tim Simms, and this is my assistant Janice Williams."

There was hugging and handshaking all around. "Now, what's the problem?" Commander Davis asked. Then walking towards the submerged Orca he continued, "Is that the one you call Mother?"

"Yes, Jill has been telecommunicating with her some," Shirley said. "But all we know is that she is clearly sick, and possibly dying. If anything, she looks like she may be starving to death."

As Chloe reached the Orca, she waded out and knelt in front of her. "Hi, Mother, remember me?" She asked, not expecting Mother to answer.

"She does recognize you," Jill said and is greeting you in her own way, which was accompanied by some quiet whistles and clicks from Mother.

"You were right, just looking at her tells me that she is considerably undernourished and obviously quite ill," Chloe observed.

"I know you just walked up, but what do you suppose could be the cause?" Jill asked as Chloe waded slowly back and forth in front of Mother.

"The usual cause of malnourishment is lack of food, the real question is, why? The obvious answer is that she is having problems with her digestive system. From what I know, Orcas are not prone to any known diseases. But that doesn't rule out that possibility.

Unlike some species of pilot whales which beach themselves for unknown reasons, Orcas do not usually do that. To start as simply as possible, let's see if I can get her to lift up a little bit and open her mouth." As she said this Chloe used her hands to attempt to open Mother's mouth.

Initially, Mother refused to open her mouth but then Jill spoke to her [Mother open mouth] and aloud for all to hear while sending what she hoped was an image of an Orca with an open mouth.

Mother shuddered a little then tilted her body lifting her head up, not completely out of the water but far enough to be able to lift her chin off the bottom a few inches then she opened her mouth a few inches.

Chloe squatted down then went to her knees to get low enough to see into Mother's mouth, but the mouth was still mostly under water and she said to Jill "I can't see anything, Jill. Can you get her to open her mouth a little farther? I need a light and a mask or goggles." She turned and shouted, "Has anybody got a good waterproof light I can use and a mask or goggles?"

"We do, Bobby." Jill said, "go over to our boat and ask Jack for both and we will see which one works best." Jill said, then shouted to Jack to give her goggles and mask to Bobby.

"Coming, Honey!" Bobby replied as he was handed a battle lantern from within the chopper then ran over to Jack who handed him the mask and goggles. Then he went over to where Chloe was examining the Orca. "Here will these do?"

Chloe took the lantern from Bobby and turned it on while looking at it. "Damn," she exclaimed as Mother reacted to the light and as she rubbed her own eyes. "How can I dim it down some so I don't scare the Orca with it?"

"Here," Bobby explained, as he adjusted the brightness. "It is usually meant to be seen in the dark from a mile away and maybe even in a storm so it is normally left set to full bright. But this model you can adjust it almost down to nothing."

"Thanks, Sweetheart, I appreciate it. Stick around in case I need to do something else" Chloe responded as she adjusted the light to what she thought would be adequate to light the inside of the Orca's mouth without frightening or blinding her.

Then she asked Jill, "Can you get her to open her mouth again only wider so I can see into it without getting salt water in my eyes?"

"Don't forget the goggles, Chloe." Bobby said.

Chloe put on the goggles and said, "Okay Jill."

Jill nodded in response and said, "[Mother open mouth] telepathically as well as aloud while trying to send an image of a gaping mouth"

Once again, the Orca lifted herself up a little and opened her mouth as before, then a little wider so that only a couple of inches was above the water line. Chloe ducked in quickly and she backed out right away and said, "I still only got a glimpse of the inside and we have to do something about her teeth." as she showed scrape marks on her chest and stomach which were oozing blood.

"I never thought of that," Jill said, then asked the group, "Do any of you have an idea about what we can do to keep the Orca's teeth from scraping Chloe as she goes in and out of the Orca's mouth?"

"How about seat cushions?" Sam suggested.

"Great idea Sam," Jill replied, "We have a couple on the boat. Would someone go and fetch two or three, please?"

"I'll go" Sam said as he took off running to the Kline's boat again.

Jack heard the request and handed two cushions to Sam who brought them back to Jill and Chloe.

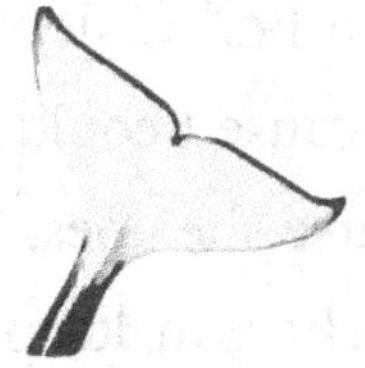

Chloe finds the Cause

Chloe positioned one of the cushions on Mother's lower teeth, took a deep breath and ducked under the water with the light and shined it into Mother's mouth and adjusted it to be a little brighter. Jill placed the other cushion on Chloe's back as Chloe began to go into Mother's mouth. In just a few seconds Chloe backed out and surfaced, shook her head and said, "Damn, I can't see much because her tongue is in the way, but just as I suspected, I felt a bunch of plastic bags on either side of and under her tongue that I could reach that could be blocking her system. Here are a couple I could reach. I think I can remove more of them but I will have to reach deeper into her mouth behind her tongue to do it. Do you think you can communicate with Mother and have her open her mouth again and let me try to remove them and not bite me. I'm going to have a problem staying under the water for any length of time, but I can definitely see much better."

"Chloe, hang on, have you ever used either a rebreather or a dive tank?"

"No, but how hard can it be?" Chloe brightened up as she asked. "That would be perfect because I could stay in her mouth as long as necessary assuming of course she doesn't decide to close her mouth. How long do you think she can keep it open? I don't think she would intentionally try to bite me but she might get tired and just close it unintentionally and cushion or not, those teeth look wicked. They are four to six inches long. What do you think Jill?"

"Hang on, one thing at a time." Jill said then turning to Sam asked, "Would you mind going over to the boat again and get my dive tanks from Jack?"

A few minutes later Sam came back with the dive tanks and said as he handed them to Jill, "Jack said the dive tanks are too big to go into her mouth and to ask you if you had ever used a snorkel, Chloe."

"Yes, lots of times as a kid at the swimming pool and sometimes in the ocean, but I don't have one anymore." Chloe replied.

"That's okay, here's one that Jack sent," Sam said as he handed the snorkel to Chloe. "It's a long one and he thought it might be easier to use than a dive tank,"

"Great idea, why didn't I think of that?" Jill exclaimed.

"That is a start, but what about something to keep her from closing her mouth and maybe even a pair of tongs so I can grab the plastic further in behind her tongue to pull it out. Then I will not need to go so deeply into her mouth." Chloe said.

"Bobby, we have a pair of barbecue tongs in the cabin," Jill said to Chloe's husband.

"On my way," Bobby said as he turned and dashed over to the boat.

"Chloe, the cushions are going to have to be what keeps her from closing her mouth for the time being unless you have some other ideas," Jill said. "I can't see putting something in her mouth to force it to stay open because she might panic and begin flailing about hurting herself and you."

"I hadn't thought about that, we will make do with the cushions and hope," Chloe said.

Bobby returned shortly with a pair of aluminum barbecue tongs and handed them to Chloe, "Here you go Babe, now is there anything else I can fetch at the moment?"

Jill laughed at his question and said, "Nothing I can think of at the moment but give us a few more minutes and I am sure something will come up."

"Jill, the bottom cushion is still in place so she doesn't seem to be troubled with that and the other cushion on top was a great idea. Can you get her to open up again and I will try it with the snorkel and see how it goes?"

"I don't know, but I'll try. This is going to need images or pictures so I probably won't be able to speak out what I tell her." Then Jill put her head against Mother's head and tried to picture an Orca opening its mouth and a person reaching into the mouth. "I have no idea how she might react, but she seemed to understand, or at least

I think she did. Good luck. I will stay in communication with her while you do it and if I say pull out do it quickly, okay?"

Chloe clears the plastic

"How am I supposed to hear you with my head inside the mouth?" Chloe asked. "Oh, what the hell. Bobby hold me from behind and if either Jill or I somehow signal to pull me out, pull fast and remember she has a whole mouth full of very sharp teeth."

"Are you nuts?" Bobby shouted.

"Maybe, but I have worked with this Orca before and I trust her. She is very weak from lack of nourishment, and I hope I am too big for her to eat. So, here's hoping!" Chloe said as she said to Jill, "Now." As she took another deep breath through the snorkel and ducked under the water as Mother opened her mouth. Jill placed the upper cushion on Chloe's back and helped ease her into the mouth.

There was not much room for Chloe to get in, but some of the plastic bag material was close to the front of the mouth along the sides of and under the tongue so she began with that, grasping what she could and handing it out of the mouth to Bobby who tossed it up on the beach. After a couple of minutes, Chloe backed out of the mouth and handed more of the plastic material to Bobby, took a few deep breaths, then went back in for more.

Chloe kept up her efforts for several more minutes and then backed out of Mother's mouth and removed the cushions. Then she reached up and patted Mother on the head and thanked her. Jill passed along the thanks and Mother once again gave forth with whistles and clicks which everyone read as gratitude.

Then Chloe gave her report. "I got everything I could see and reach but there could still be more in there. I was able to reach to the back of her tongue and I got some from there. My biggest concern is that there might still be some at her pharynx which is at the tongue end of the esophagus. It is very muscular and generally propels the food into the esophagus which conveys it to the stomach system. If it is not too much and we can get her to eat, the food it could push it into her stomach where it might dissolve in the stomach acids. Orca stomach acids should be pretty strong as it enables the orcas here in the Puget Sound area to eat mostly salmon whole. Sorry for the makeshift Orca anatomy lesson but I needed to go over it in my head. That helped me visualize the anatomy but she needs food.

"Now, how can we feed her? I think she may be too weak to feed herself right now, and I can't see us trying to feed her whole salmon which is her main food source. They eat from 100 to 300 pounds of food per day depending on their size and what is available to them. In her case the primary food is salmon and which kind depends, I suppose, on what is available at the time. Around here I suspect it would probably be King Salmon or Silvers."

"How about if we get some ground-up salmon for her?" Janice asked. "Are there any canneries around here?"

"I'll check," Bobby responded as he pulled out his cell phone and began searching. Shortly he reported. "There are between 20 and 30 canneries in the area according to Google."

"Why don't you let me check into this for you? What do you think you need?" Commander Davis asked.

"My guess would be 100 pounds or so of whatever they have. King would be best because it is the oiliest and oil is what I suspect she needs the most. Oh, and it will have to be raw, not cooked." Chloe replied.

"Okay Chloe, give me a few minutes." Commander Davis replied as he walked back to the Coast Guard helicopter.

Half an hour later he returned looking hopeful. "I called several canneries before I found one that had received a fresh haul recently. I told several of them what you needed and most of them took the attitude to just let her die because Orcas eat too much salmon reducing their catch. Finally, I got one man, a Mr. Juan Alverez, who admired Orcas even though they eat his salmon, and he had just received a fresh catch. He said he would grind up a hundred pounds or so and bring it right over in about an hour. I'm supposed to call him back and tell him how we are going to feed it to the Orca."

Chloe looked up at him and said, "I haven't the slightest idea how to feed her. Any suggestions?" She looked around at the group hopefully. "From what little I know about how their alimentary canal works the mouth is the obvious entry point then comes the pharynx which is the organ between the mouth and the esophagus. Her pharynx is right at the back of her tongue, but it is effectively a valve to control what is passed along. So, I guess the best we could do is to somehow get the salmon to the back of her tongue and hope she recognizes it and opens the pharynx to let the food pass."

"Shouldn't you put some of it on her tongue so she could taste it and decide to eat it? Chloe?" Shirley asked.

"Probably. But, there is some doubt that Orcas can actually taste their food. Some species have been found to have the equivalent of taste buds on their tongues, but I have no idea whether Mother is one of those."

"Then how do they decide what to eat?" Shirley asked.

"My best guess is their eyes determine what they try to catch, and they bite it before they try to swallow it and the tongue is rough. Somehow, they must do something to reduce the size of, for example, a large King Salmon so it can be passed by the pharynx into the esophagus and ultimately to the stomach. People do the same thing; we have a pharynx which is supposed to keep us from choking on our food. Anything too big we just can't swallow, I suspect the same thing is probably true of Orcas. From what I have read, Orcas eat their food in chunks or entirely whole."

"Commander, would you please call him back and tell him what I just said about how Orcas feed. Maybe he could bring some whole salmon and we could see if she would eat them, if so the problem is solved, if not then we will have to discuss how to make the food more edible for her.

"Right, but maybe you should be in on the call don't you think?"

"You're right let's go" Chloe and the Commander stepped away from the group for quiet and called Mr. Alverez back.

"Mr. Alverez, I am Coast Guard Commander Richard Davis, we spoke a little while ago about feeding an Orca."

"I remember you Commander, have you decided how you are going to feed the Orca?"

"We have just been discussing that. I have Dr. Chloe Archer of the Oregon Institute of Marine Studies with me and after a very detailed discussion with Dr. Archer about how Orca's eat, we are not too sure what to ask for nor how to give it to her."

"Yeah, I looked into that as well. Your idea of grinding it into a slurry didn't ring quite well with me. What would keep it from coming right back out of the mouth?"

"You're right Mr. Alverez. Dr. Archer came to essentially the same conclusion so what do you suggest?"

"Commander, Mr. Alverez was my father, just call me Juan. I'm bringing some salmon that were caught today, so they will be essentially fresh. I'll be there in a few minutes."

Dinner is served

Five minutes later a well-used rusty pickup truck turned onto the beach and drove over to the group with the Orca. An older man stepped out of the truck and extended his hand to Commander Davis. "Hi Commander, I'm Juan Alverez and there are your fish" he said pointing to the bed of the pickup.

"Welcome, Juan, my name is Richard, and this is Dr. Chloe Archer." Commander Davis said indicating Chloe. "The rest of the folks are people who have worked with the Orcas before, including this specific Orca. They came to try to rescue Mother, as they call her because she is the mother of a pod."

"Hello, folks, call me Juan. As I told Richard, I brought a couple of bushels of small to medium-sized salmon that were freshly caught today. I can't say that any of them are still alive but some may be. From what I read Orcas come up behind a school of salmon or whatever species are running and scoop them up from behind. Whether they bite them or just suck them in by opening their mouths probably depends on the size of the catch. Whatever it is and how it is processed, it ultimately ends up on the tongue which must do something to them to pass the fish back to the throat, which has a really strange name. I didn't read anything that said what Orcas do after the fish is on the tongue. I suspect that they may press the catch to the roof of their mouth and maybe scrape the catch with their tongues which have a rough texture according to the stuff I found on the internet. Why not just toss them into her mouth onto her tongue and see what she does with them? As salmon are typically caught from behind but I would throw them in head first and start at the front of her tongue, and see how that works."

"Mr. Alverez, Juan, that is the best way I ever read or heard it described. I think you have hit it right on the head. Would you like to throw the first fish into her mouth to see what happens?" Chloe asked.

"Thank you, Dr. Archer, Chloe, I would relegate that honor to you and your team. But I would be glad to watch, and I will supply as much salmon as you need." Mr. Alverez said. "I'll get the fish." As he said this Alverez walked back over to his truck, folded back a tarp, and uncovered a bushel basket full of fish out of it.

"Hang on Juan, I will be right over to help you," Bobby said as he began running over to the truck.

"Thank you, son, it is really heavy, and I brought several baskets after I found out how much an Orca can eat per day."

Alverez on one side and Bobby Archer on the other they carried the basket full of salmon over to where Mother was lying. "Here you go for starters Dr. Archer. Archer?" He asked looking around at Bobby."

"My wife, sir," Bobby said with a smile.

"Thank you, Juan, and please call me Chloe and as you have guessed Bobby is my husband, he also flies that helicopter over there for the Coast Guard. This is Jill Kline and her husband Jack and my assistant Janice. Jill is psychic and she can communicate with the Orca. And those two over there are Sylvia and Sam Worther."

"Pleased to meet you, folks. I think what you are doing is just great or as my father would say, Mui Bueno." Juan said as he shook hands with everyone.

"Let's get to it folks," Chloe said as she took two salmon from the basket. "Jill, ask her to open her mouth again, please."

"Righto," Jill said as she put her head against Mother's head and said [Open Mouth].

Mother opened her mouth again and Chloe carefully tossed the two salmon onto the middle of Mother's tongue. Mother waited a moment and then closed her mouth, and almost immediately re-opened her mouth with her tongue in view and the salmon were gone. Mother clicked and chittered.

Mother is greatful

Jill looked up at Chloe with tears in her eyes. "She is grateful for the food, I think she is really grateful and from what she is sending would like some more."

The whole team raised a cheer and Mr Alverez moved the basket over next to Chloe.

No sooner had she given Mother some of the fish than first one and soon many seagulls showed up overhead and began screeching and calling. Seconds later one of the gulls swooped down and picked up one of the smaller salmon right out of the basket and tried to fly away. Several others chased after the thief. The rest circled overhead screeching and screaming getting ready to raid the basket.

At about the same time, a boat went by in the channel and honked its horn a couple of times, and waved at the group on the beach. Commander Davis waved back at them, as they went on their way.

"If you folks will excuse me, I think I will wander over to Jack's boat, I think there might be too many people here right now," Sam said.

"You may be right Sam, thanks for being so considerate," Chloe said.

"I'd go and get the tarp from the truck to cover the basket but that would just leave the baskets on the truck open to the gulls." Mr. Alverez said. "What can we do to protect the basket while Chloe feeds the Orca?"

Chloe shooed away the incoming gulls and took two more salmon and tossed them into Mother's mouth and again Mother closed her mouth and apparently ate them then reopened her mouth asking for more.

"Just a minute guys," Bobby said, "How about covering the basket with one of the cushions?" Which he did.

As Chloe went back and forth to the basket she had to lift the cushion to get at the salmon and had to shoo away the gulls one of which actually tried to land on her head and was chased away by

Bobby. Chloe kept this up until the entire basket of fish was consumed. She then took a break.

Mother continued to make Orca sounds of clicking and chittering and opened her mouth again.

Mother asks for more

"I think she wants more, Chloe," Jill said.

"I'll bet she does," Chloe said with a big grin on her face. "Mr. Alverez, did you say you had some more?"

"I sure did. Bobby, let's go get another basket." Alverez said as he headed for his truck.

"Right behind you sir," Bobby said as he followed him back to the truck.

They carried the second basket over and placed it beside Chloe.

"Chloe," Juan said. "Do you think it is wise to give her so much so soon after getting her started?"

"Well, she is asking for it so I don't know what else to do. What do you think is the worst thing that could happen?" Chloe asked.

"Well, I don't have any experience with Orcas, but when starving people are presented with a lot of food they tend to try and eat it all and typically make themselves sick and throw it all back up. Like I said, I have no idea whether what you gave her was a banquet, a meal, or an appetizer."

"I never thought about that, Juan." Chloe replied, then asked Jill, "What do you think Jill, do you suppose we should go slow and see what happens?"

"Your guess is better than mine," Jill replied. "But it shouldn't be a big deal to wait an hour or two to see how she reacts to what she's had so far. I'll try talking to her and see what reaction I get. I read somewhere that like Mr. Alverez said, they can eat up to 300 pounds of fish in a day.

"How about we have something to eat while we are waiting, huh? Juan if you will drive I would be happy to buy a couple of pizzas." Commander Davis said then added. "How about thin crust pepperoni and sausage, any objections? Oh, and some very cold soft drinks and water?"

"Sounds great Commander," Jill said. "Any objections?"

There were assorted comments all of which were in favor.

"Let's go, Commander," Juan said. "But first could we offload the last basket of salmon to keep them from either tipping or bouncing out while we go?"

"Got it," Bobby said as he gestured to Tim to join him. The two of them lifted the third basket of salmon off the truck. "Juan, can we take the tarp to cover the baskets to keep the gulls off and so the fish don't spoil?"

"Certainly," Juan said as he folded the tarp and handed it to Tim. "I'll be back in less than an hour. I need to stop by my company and let the staff know where I am and what I am doing which should only take a few minutes. I'll order the pizza on the way and pick it up when I am finished at the company, okay?"

"Okay," Bobby replied. "Come on Tim, let's get back to the folks."

"Hey, wait a minute Juan, are you going anywhere near the marina?" Sam asked.

"I go right by it," Juan replied.

"Would you mind dropping me off so I can get my boat and bring it up here?"

"Not at all. Come on." Juan replied as Commander Davis opened the passenger side door to let Sam in."

Enter The News

As Juan was about to drive off, another helicopter arrived overhead and hovered about a hundred feet above the Orca and the people near her. From above came a voice, "Hello, ladies and gentlemen, we are from Channel Five News. Someone called and told us you were helping an injured Orca. We've come to see what you are doing with the Orca, so we can show it on the evening news."

Chloe muttered various expletives under her breath, then shouted to Commander Davis, "Can you deal with them, Commander, please? They are frightening Mother, and we have enough on our hands right now without having to deal with a helicopter and the news."

"Sure, Chloe. Sorry fellows, I need to drop out to handle this. Here is some money to pay for the pizzas." Commander Davis said, offering some cash to Juan.

"Keep it, Commander," Sam interjected before Juan could reply. "I'll take care of the pizzas, and it looks like we had better buy a couple more as well."

"Thanks, Sam," Commander Davis said, then nodding to Chloe added. "Dr. Archer, I am afraid there is no way to make them go away. They have every right to capture news as it happens if they can. I can see that Mother is not reacting well to their noise. I will ask them to land up the beach on the other side of our chopper and honor your need for, shall we call it, security. I don't want to pull rank on them, but if necessary, I can."

"Okay, Commander. Can they limit the observers to just one close to us, please? Mother reacted to the noise and downdraft and Jill is still trying to calm her down again."

"I will see that they do and try to keep them at a distance. But, to be fair, they will have questions. Would you be amenable to answering some questions, Chloe?"

"Let me finish with this basket first. Okay?" Chloe requested.

"Okay. I'd better get over there now before they come over here. I will explain what you are doing as best I can before I bring them over." Commander Davis finished.

Commander Davis got to the front of the Coast Guard helicopter just as the TV crew was coming around it. "Hi, folks, I am Coast Guard Commander Richard Davis, and I am acting to protect what is going on at the other end of this beach. I am prepared to answer any questions you might have."

"Thank you, Commander, I am Virginia Grant, a producer for Channel 5 News, and this is our human-interest team. Someone called us and reported that some people were harassing an Orca near the Kelp Forest area. So, we came up to see what you were up to and to report what you were doing. Considering that you are here, I hardly think that you people were harassing the animal. But unfortunately, they did not report that the Coast Guard was here. So, Commander, could you tell us to the camera, please, exactly what is happening here and why the Coast Guard is involved? And, before you start, wasn't there a similar event a couple of years ago that the Coast Guard also participated in?"

"Beginning with your last question first, yes, there was a similar event about two years ago in which Captain, now Admiral Miller, and crew from the Port Angeles Coast Guard Station participated. It is fairly common for the Coast Guard to become involved in these kinds of problems because we work closely with the National Oceanic and Atmospheric Administration when called upon. That event involved assisting a juvenile Orca which had been deliber-ately run over by a fishing boat and seriously injured. This event happens to involve the mother of that Orca. She is starving because she ingested some plastic bags discarded in the area waters by some careless individuals. The bags have blocked her digestive system, so she could not ingest her normal sustenance."

"Thank you, Commander. Can you tell us how it happens that the Orca assisted two years ago is involved in this event?

"Yes, I think so. From what I have been told, the juvenile, who we have nick-named Sonny, sought out the people who helped him by trying to find their boat out in the Strait. He did find a similar boat and deliberately bumped it to get the owners' attention. Those boat owners, Sam and Sylvia Worther, were aware of the rules about Orca contact, so they called the Washington Division of Fish and

Wildlife and reported the incident to Warden Shirley White, the woman over there in the brown uniform." He said, pointing at the group around the Orca. "She was involved in the earlier incident with the juvenile and suspected that he was trying to contact the same people who had helped him. So, Ms. White, with the concurrence of her supervisor, contacted the people who helped with the earlier incident. They are Jack and Jill Kline. At Shirley's request, they brought their boat up to the area and went looking for Sonny. After a short search either they found Sonny or he found them. Sonny led them over to where the female, his mother, who is also the pod leader, was stranded in the shallow water just off this beach."

"Did you get all of that guys?" Ms. Grant asked the camera man and recorder.

"Yes, Ma'am. We got it all." Her assistant replied.

Then she continued, "Thank you, Commander. That was a very concise and complete description of the situation."

"There's more," Commander Davis continued. "In the incident two years ago, Ms. White's WDFW chief called a relative of his who is an aquatic animal veterinarian from the Oregon Institute of Marine Studies in Portland and they arranged through Admiral Miller, the Port Angeles Coast Guard Station Commander, to have a helicopter from my station in Oregon fly the Vet and his assistant up to the site of the incident where they treated the juvenile Orca and apparently healed his wounds.

When Ms. White took over the management of this event, she called the Oregon Institute for help and while the Vet who came up two years ago was no longer there, his assistant who was instrumental in treating the juvenile two years ago was available and she, Dr. Chloe Archer, who is a fully qualified marine mammal veterinarian and is the one over there feeding the now able to eat mother Orca.

"A few words about why we are here. When Ms. White called Dr. Archer, Dr. Archer called me about getting a ride up here from Portland. Because of our previous assistance, I agreed. That, plus the fact that my Chief, Pilot, Lt. Robert Archer, is now Dr. Archer's husband. They were married about a year ago."

"Now, let's wander over there and see what they are doing. Please do not go rushing over there because you might frighten the Orca and undo everything that has been done so far. Understood?"

"Yes, sir, understood." Ms. Grant said, then added to her team, "Everything in moderation, guys. I am confident that we will get plenty of opportunities to record the proceedings. Record me speaking with Dr. Archer and the others but maintain your distance. I would hate to undo all they have done just to get a story. I think there is plenty of story for us without that. Okay?"

"Okay, ma'am." They replied in chorus.

"If you would be so kind as to lead the way and handle the introductions as appropriate, Commander Davis, we would appreciate it."

As they were finishing the discussion with Commander Davis, Juan's pickup truck drove quietly onto the beach and down to where the caretakers were working around the Orca.

"Hello, all," Juan said as he exited the truck. "Chloe, I brought some more salmon for you and four pizzas for everybody."

"Thanks, Juan," Chloe said, then added, "Come on guys let's us eat too."

"How would you folks like a slice of pizza, Ms. Grant?" Commander Davis asked the TV producer. "Follow me, please. I'm sure there will be more than enough, and it will give you and your team an opportunity to meet Doctor Archer's team and the rest of the crew."

Enter the News

Commander Davis led the TV crew over to where Juan was parking his truck after backing it up toward the group around Mother.

"Hi, Commander!" Juan said. "How about some pizza?"

"Sounds great, Juan. I have a few more guests for lunch." Commander Davis said, then added. "Attention, everybody. This is Virginia Grant and her crew from Channel 5 News. They are here to see what you are doing to, for, or with the Orca."

"Hi, folks. Please don't mind us. We will do our best to keep out of your way. After what Commander Davis has told us, we are confident that what you are doing is beneficial to the Orca. We want to get the story so our audience can see how beneficial your efforts are to the Orca, who, Commander Davis told us, is known to you as Mother.

"Dr. Archer, if you have a moment or two after you finish your pizza, please fill us in on what you have done and are doing.

Chloe handed the rest of her piece of pizza to her husband and said, "I'd be delighted to answer any questions you might have, Virginia."

"Commander Davis has filled us in on some of the details of what you do and how you are doing it. But, first, how did you remove the plastic trash from the Orca?"

"Ms. Jill Kline, come here Jill, is able to communicate with the Orca and got her to open her mouth," Chloe replied.

"Communicated with her?" Virginia asked, looking at Jill with eyebrows raised, "how were you able to do that? Or, should I ask?"

"Oh, you can ask, but I am not sure you will believe the answer, so I suggest you stop recording while I tell you," Jill replied.

Virginia turned to her crew with a wink and said, "Take five guys. Go have some pizza."

"Okay, boss." The cameraman said, and he put down his camera so it was pointing at Jill and Chloe, and the sound man did the same with his equipment. Then they walked over to join the rest of the crowd around Juan's truck.

"My husband and I are mutually telepathic." Jill began.

"Telepathic, like you can read minds and stuff?" Virginia asked disbelievingly.

"Well, yes. We often communicate silently with each other, but it is not general, which is to say, I cannot read or communicate with your mind or anyone else's, which you will disbelieve when you hear what I have to say next. But could you please turn off your camera and recording equipment which were left conveniently pointing in our direction and are still recording. How I know this is not by reading your mind, but because the active light on the camera is still lit, and I assume that is true for the microphone as well." Jill said with emphasis. "We do not wish to have our ability exposed to the TV audience for obvious reasons, and if you do reveal it, we will sue you and the station. Understood?"

At this moment, Jack walked up to the group, picked up the camera and microphone, found the on-off switches, and turned them off.

"Understood!" Virginia reacted, then continued. "Now, how did you do it, and what can I say about it?"

"Let's just say the power of suggestion got Mother to open her mouth. Chloe, Dr. Archer, tried to open Mother's mouth with her hands and was initially unsuccessful. After several tries and with my assistance, Mother eventually cooperated and opened her mouth. After that, Chloe reached into the mouth and removed some of the plastic within easy reach. In the process, she, Dr. Archer, was scraped by Mother's bottom teeth, which are razor sharp. Then, to reach the rest of the plastic bags, Dr. Archer tried to open Mother's mouth further. Mother finally opened as wide as she could, we think, and Dr. Ascher covered Mother's teeth, top and bottom, with boat cushions and actually crawled into the mouth and removed what we are pretty sure was the rest of the plastic."

"Unfortunately, when Chloe finished removing the plastic bags and stuff, we were pretty sure Mother did not have enough strength to feed herself. We debated on what and how we could feed her and settled on ground salmon. Commander Davis called several local canning plants looking for a source of salmon. The result was Mr.

Juan Alverez of Alverez Sea Harvest arrived with three baskets of fresh caught salmon. He, Mr. Alverez, didn't think our idea of using ground or pureed salmon was such a good idea because that is different from how orcas feed. We discussed how to go about feeding Mother and settled on having her open her mouth and have Chloe toss in two salmon onto Mother's tongue. Mother closed her mouth and, a minute or two later, opened it again without prompting, and the salmon was gone. We continued doing that for two bushel baskets of salmon, after which Mother rested for a few minutes. Then she asked for more by opening her mouth, clicking, and making Orca sounds. We were a little nervous about feeding her more, fearing it might be too much, but we fed them to her anyway. Now she is resting.

"Mr. Alverez brought two more baskets of fish when he brought the pizza, but we think we should wait until tomorrow to give her some time to process what she has eaten already."

"Dr. Archer, how long do you think it will be before Mother can fend for herself?" Virginia asked.

"I would guess maybe a week. She was pretty weak when we got here. My guess is that if we had been much later, she would not have survived. Even now, we have our fingers crossed that she will recover. We will have more salmon to feed her tomorrow, thanks to Mr. Alverez and a couple of other friendly fisheries." Chloe replied.

"Dr. Archer, and Commander Davis, do either of you object to having your names mentioned when we show our report on what you have been doing and hope to accomplish?" Virginia asked.

"Chloe, why don't you go first," Commander Davis offered.

Chloe's Story

"I have no objection if it is quoted accurately and not sensation-alized, at least from our perspective," Chloe replied. "What we have been doing in effect is assisting an animal in distress. In that sense, we are not doing any more than anyone else trying to help an injured animal. We recognize that Orcas have a special place in the hearts of many people, especially in this area. We also realize that they are often a nuisance to sport fishermen when they literally steal the fish right off the fishermen's lines as they reel in their catch.

"I would appreciate it very much if you would focus on the cause of this event, quite literally the disposing of waste, especially plastic bags and wrappings in the seas, the straits, and other local waters where marine animals like the Orcas, various species of whales, sea lions, seals and otters to name just a few, can ingest the trash and die horrible deaths of starvation and asphyxiation or even poisoning.

"This Orca, which we have called Mother, because she is in fact, the Mother of another Orca that was deliberately run over by a pair of fishermen two years ago and whom we treated for rather serious injuries he incurred because of that event.

"He sought out and contacted several boaters who ignored it and did not report the contact. We know that because several volunteer Orca watchers reported the contacts to the authorities. In this instance, those who did not call the WDFW were not cited because the Orca came to them, so they could not avoid it.

"Finally, he approached Mr. and Mrs. Sam Worther, who dutifully contacted the WDFW reporting the contact to WDFW Warden Shirley White, as required by law. If Sam and Sylvia had not reported their contact, we would not be here today, and Mother would probably be dead.

"We are only here because of that event. She, whom we call Mother, is the Mother of the injured Orca we have dubbed Sonny from two years ago and who searched for and found someone to come and help his Mother, who is the leader of the pod. He approached the Worthers because their boat closely resembles the boat of Mr. and Mrs. Jack Kline which is over there on the beach. The Klines were instrumental in the treatment and recovery of Sonny, and as you can probably see, they have decals and a flag on their boat that entitles them to be in close contact with the Orcas.

"The Worthers called WDFW and spoke with Shirley White, who contacted the Klines who came up to Everett, where they met Shirley and the Worthers and who were guided to Mother by Sonny. After they found Mother, they contacted me because the Institute I work for is the one which treated Sonny's injuries in the past. Then I called the Coast Guard and asked them if they could fly me up here the same way they did when we treated Sonny. So here I am. Since then, it has been pretty touch and go as we tried to diagnose what was wrong with Mother, which was starvation because of the plastic she got into her mouth, which blocked her ability to ingest her food."

"With much help, I was able to remove the plastic, and thanks to Commander Davis, who found Mr. Alverez, who brought several bushels of freshly caught salmon, we have been able to feed Mother and hopefully begin to restore her to the ability to feed herself again. Although it will probably take several more days before she can fend for herself, Mr. Alverez has assured us that there will be fresh salmon available as long as needed from his company and several others he has contacted."

"Okay, everybody, have I left out anything important or even anything trivial?" Chloe asked, then continued, "You should ask Commander Davis and Mr. Alverez for their inputs as well."

"Thank you, Dr. Archer, that was quite interesting, and I might add a thorough story about the situation and what you are doing to rectify it," Virginia said. "Now, Commander Davis, what could you add to this situation from the Coast Guard point of view?"

Commander Davis explains

Commander Davis paused for a few moments to consider his comments, then began, "I have known Dr. Archer for over a year ever since she and Lieutenant Robert Archer, my most senior rescue helicopter pilot, fell in love and got married after meeting up here about two years ago during another rescue of an Orca in distress.

"In truth, Ms. Grant, there is not much I can add to Dr. Archer's rather thorough description of why we all are here and what we are doing. As you may know, the Coast Guard works closely with the National Oceanographic and Atmospheric Administration and local authorities like the Washington Division of Fish and Wildlife in support of their activities, which include monitoring interactions between humans and sea life. Admiral Miller set the boundaries of what we might do concerning the Orcas and other sea life in and around the Pacific Northwest, especially in the straits and estuarial waters.

"As Dr. Archer said, we are here because she called for help rescuing an Orca in distress. Ordinarily, we would not have heard of this incident if we had not been called and asked for help. I am grateful that we were available and not otherwise occupied when we were called to help by ferrying Dr. Archer and her assistant up here.

"We have had wonderful assistance in treating the Orca from Mr. Alverez and some of his friends who have contributed lots of salmon, with which to feed the Orca.

"Now, may I ask that you not reveal where we are and why we are here? That includes all of us because the worst thing that could happen now would be for many people to come here to see what we are doing and ruin the entire effort by causing the Orca to panic and try to escape and possibly drown and almost certainly die of starvation."

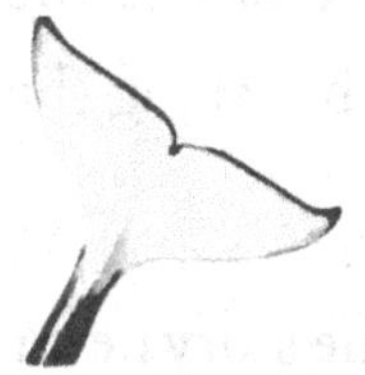

News Agrees to Limit Story

"I understand, Commander, but we have a job to do just like you do. We would like to take some pictures of everyone, some video and recordings, etc. If we wait several days, say until our human interest program on Sunday morning before doing our report, do you think that would be long enough? That's only four days. Face it, by this time. The word could be out to other media teams from well-meaning people who like to get recognition for reporting events like this. I put it that way because there are bound to be other media teams who will find out one way or another and want to scoop us with their report."

"Just a minute, Ms. Grant, let me confer with Dr. Archer to see what she thinks."

"Okay, Commander, I will wait right here." Ms. Grant replied.

Commander Davis walked over to where Chloe was feeding more salmon to Mother and asked her, "Dr. Archer, er, Chloe, how long do you think it will be before you are through with Mother? Ms, Grant wants to know how long she has to wait before going on the air with the story."

"I'd be just as happy if the story never went out. It didn't last time, you know." Chloe replied.

"That's not entirely true, Chloe. It made the news several weeks after the event when the boat drivers were tried in court for deliberately injuring an Orca. It was also reported on TV, but without any pictures except for a couple of photographs taken at a distance from other boats and an airplane from above. Didn't you know that?" Commander Davis said.

"No, sir, I didn't know that. By then, I was back in Portland working on my thesis, and Dr. Goodhurst never mentioned it. I think I knew about the airplane because it circled overhead for a while. but then someone else was in charge.

"Anyway, I guess there is no getting around it, is there, sir?" Chloe finished.

"No, I am afraid not. So let's make the best of it. Ms. Grant says she can probably wait until Sunday to release it unless another newsgroup gets word of it, then she will have to report it too." Commander Davis replied.

"Okay. Now when will Mother be ready to try life on her own again? My best guess is a couple more days. She is starting to fill out again, so the food is helping to speed her recovery, and as far as I can tell, her other bodily functions are working again. My best guess is, she will begin to have signs of independence, probably in two days and hopefully, be ready to go it on her own by the week-end. Her strength is coming back because now she can move her flukes up and down, and she backed up a couple of feet into slightly deeper water. I am still feeding her and will as long as she needs me or will let me. Oh, hell, here comes another truck or van. I hope it is one of Mr. Alverez's friends."

Channel 13 News

Commander Davis turned to see the incoming van and swore quietly to himself. The sign on the side of the van said Channel 13. It was obviously another media team. He and Ms. Grant walked over to the van. "Hi, folks. What can we do for you?" He asked.

"Hi, Virginia, fancy meeting you here." the driver said, ignoring Commander Davis' greeting.

"Hi, Dave," she replied. "What are you doing here?"

"The same thing you are, I suspect, looking for a story." The driver replied, still ignoring Commander Davis.

"Commander Davis of the Coast Guard, this is David McCoy from channel 13," Virginia made the introductions.

"Nice to meet you, sir," Dave replied, finally offering Commander Davis his hand.

Commander Davis shook Dave's hand and said. "I am in command here at the request of the WDFW. We are in the process of assisting in the rescue of a stranded and injured Orca, and I ask you to respect the situation and do nothing to interfere with the effort."

"Yes, sir Commander. We just want to see what is going on so we can report it in our human-interest program, Do you have any objections? If you do, I am prepared to contact the station's attorney."

Commander Davis took a deep breath, then said, "Is it necessary to take that sort of attitude, Mr. McCoy? I have no objection to your being here and watching what the people here are doing. I was just cautioning you to keep your distance from the people who are working with the Orca. She, the Orca, is in distress and could panic if she or the people helping her are disturbed."

"Take it easy, Dave. No one wants to keep you from recording what is happening as long as it is from a distance." Virginia said. "I have agreed to the same terms and have recorded some of the activities. But the number of people allowed to go in close proximity of the Orca is very limited."

"What's wrong with her anyway, if I may ask?" Dave asked, still in a defensive tone.

Commander Davis nodded to Virginia, "Why don't you tell him, Virginia."

For the next ten minutes, Virginia gave a very thorough description of what was wrong with Mother, what Dr. Archer and the others were doing with Mother to help her recover, and why access to the scene had to be limited.

"Well, you got here and got your videos and stuff, didn't you?" Dave asked.

"Actually, Dave, no. Oh, I got hardly any video and only a few recordings of Commander Davis, and myself with the veterinarian, Dr. Chloe Archer, while she tried to explain what she was doing. Then Commander Davis or his chief pilot took our camera and voice recorder and turned them off. I did get some additional voice stuff on my cell phone recorder of me and some of the others. But that is all." Virginia finished.

"They can't do that, Virginia, and you know it. What about freedom of the press and all that?" Dave asked.

"Dave, my team, and I have been here for several hours. I have been allowed several times to get closer to where I could see what they were doing and talked briefly with Dr. Archer. And, if you are patient, you might be able to do the same. You, we, just cannot make a circus out of it, or it could ruin everything if the Orca becomes frightened and either dies or tries to escape before she recovers, which would more than likely have the same result."

Channel 13 meets Chloe

"Commander Davis, can you arrange for Dave to go over and see what is going on? It looks to me as if Dr. Archer is feeding Mother again. Could we sneak up behind her but not too close and give Dave some idea of what she is doing?"

"I think that can be arranged, but no video or audio recording equipment can be allowed to get too close." Commander Davis replied.

"Why not?" Dave asked.

"Because they might look or sound frightening to the Orca." Commander Davis replied. "The only people who are close up are known to the Orca because she contacted them to help treat her seriously injured son two years ago: the veterinarian, Dr. Chloe Archer, and her assistant, and the WDFW warden."

"Contacted them? How? Dave retorted.

"It's a long story. Suffice it to be accepted and NOT reported in any way to protect the contact's privacy and future interactions between humans and Orcas. As far as the world is concerned, she was found stranded on the beach here by some people who knew what to do and called a WDFW warden who knew who to call for help because of the previous event and let it go at that."

Dave started to bristle again, but Virginia intervened.

Virginia Offers to Share

"I'll tell you what, Dave," Virginia began, "I will share the video and audio I have recorded so far with you. I don't expect to get any more until maybe when the Orca is ready to leave if she does. If there is more, I will include that as well. But this cannot be released until they have finished here, understand?"

"You're serious, aren't you?" Dave was surprised.

"Yes, I am. I have seen what these people have been and are doing, and it is almost miraculous. One of the people over there can communicate with the Orca to a limited extent, and that is how they have been able to help treat her. Believe it or not, it is working. When I got here, she was all but dead. Now she is beginning to show signs of life and communicates with her actions when she needs food and when she doesn't. We should be able to go over there in a few minutes to watch the end of the current feeding.

Although when I first got here, she looked like a large, deflated balloon, she is beginning to show signs of recovery after only two days. The hope is that by this weekend, she can go out on her own and return to her pod. Did I mention that she is the Mother and leader of the pod? Look out to the Strait over there, and you will see several other Orcas swimming back and forth, awaiting her return."

"I'll be damned," Dave said as he turned and looked toward the water. "Okay, I'll play ball, but others will arrive soon because the guy who called us probably also called several others. He was disappointed when I told him that we did not give rewards for human interest calls. I told him that nobody else does either, but I don't think he believed me."

"Commander, Dave is concerned that there could have been other stations called who might send out crews. Can something be done to prevent them from coming out onto the beach and causing havoc with what is being done here?" Virginia asked.

"I don't know." Commander Davis said. "I am from Oregon and don't know any of the local commanders. I'll go over and check with Shirley White. She is the woman in the WDFW Warden uniform. She might have some idea what resources are available for crowd control."

He walked over to where Shirley was standing and said, "Shirley, what can we do to keep more people from coming out on the beach and interfering in what the folks are doing? Do you have any connections with local law enforcement or other wardens who could act as guards to prevent access to the beach?"

"No, Commander, that is not the kind of work game wardens do. Believe me, at times, I wish it was." She replied. "What about using your guys, Rob and Tim, and maybe a couple of the media people to man the entrance and prevent more people from coming out here? If we don't everything could end up being a waste of time if Mother is frightened by others before Chloe and company have finished."

"Great idea, Shirley." Commander Davis said, then he turned to Rob and Tim. "Would you two and a couple of the media folks please block the entrance? You two are in uniform, so you take charge."

"Sir, yes, sir. C'mon, Tim let's go be Guards of the Coast, at least this local coast. You go round up the two guys who came with Virginia and any who came with the new guy and we are going to block the entrance to the beach to prevent others from coming out to see what is going on," Robby Archer said.

Media to Get a View

When Commander Davis returned to where Virginia and Dave were waiting, Virginia asked, "What about the media people who are here now? Can we at least be given an opportunity to observe what is happening and maybe take some photographs? What if we use our cell phone cameras to take pictures instead of the high-tech stuff. Hell, most of what is shown on the media these days of local events is captured with some yokel's cell phone camera, isn't it?"

"That's a great idea. Virginia." Commander Davis replied. " The folks who have been working with Mother are all taking a break over there, so I suspect Mother is not eating at the moment and is resting. So if you want to go over and take a look, come with me. Shirley was involved in the Orca rescue two years ago, so she would more than likely be able to act as a guide. Please do exactly what she says and nothing more. If your cell phone cameras have flash capability, please turn it off."

Virginia and Dave followed Commander Davis over to where the others were sitting on the beach eating cold pizza. "Dr. Archer, and Ms. White, I know you met Virginia a while ago. She has been very cooperative with us and has been joined by Dave McCoy, who I think some of you may have met a while ago. They have teamed up as the TV crew and have agreed to share their efforts to minimize the amount of media interference. Could you please fill them in on what you have been doing and what is left to do if possible?"

Shirley stepped up, shook hands with both of them, and then turned to the others around the scene and explained what was happening. "This is Dr. Chloe Archer, a veterinarian from the Oregon Institute of Marine Studies. She is our specialist in charge of treating Mother. Dr. Archer was one of the vets who came up here to work on an injured young Orca two years ago. Chloe, would you like to introduce the rest of the team and explain what you all are doing?".

"It would be my pleasure, Shirley," Chloe responded. "First, let me introduce Mother, as we call her, the party's star." Chloe said, pointing to Mother, who appeared to be resting quietly. "Next, this is Jill Kline. I met Jill and her husband Jack two years ago when they encountered Mother out in the Strait off Sequim when Mother sought help for her son who was injured by malicious boaters and was in intense pain. Jill has a certain rapport with Mother and has been invaluable in assisting and guiding her treatment."

"Then, the lovely lady with mud on her face is Sylvia Worther. Sonny recruited her and her husband while they were fishing in the Strait near Everett. They reported the encounter as required by law, but they were the only ones who did. They called WDFW and told Shirley about the encounter. Take over, Shirley."

"After they called me, I thought something was amiss, so I called Jack and Jill Kline and asked them to come up here and see if they could find out what Sonny was trying to do. So they drove up here and launched their boat in Everett. We all set to go out looking for Sonny when he found them at the marina and led them to this beach where his Mother was dying of starvation."

"It didn't take long to discover the problem, after which I called The Oregon Institute for Marine Studies, looking for the veterinarian who had helped us before. But he was no longer there, and Chloe Archer, who was here with him two years ago, was his replacement. Because of her previous experience, she did not think we were nuts and arranged to come up here by calling the Coast Guard to see if she could get a helicopter ride instead of having to drive. It didn't hurt that she had married the chief Coast Guard helicopter pilot who asked his boss, Commander Davis who is standing next to you if they could go and he said yes, so here we are."

"I would also like to introduce Mr. Juan Alverez, who has provided several hundred pounds of salmon which we needed to bring Mother back from the brink of starvation because she had ingested some plastic bags and trash some careless boater dumped into the waters of the Strait."

"That's about it, Questions?" Shirley asked.

"When do you think you will be finished?" Dave asked.

Chloe stopped to think for a minute before responding. Then replied, "By the weekend, I hope. She seems to be gaining strength as we go."

Dave and Virginia spoke quietly to each other briefly then Virginia replied. "That was a very thorough description of what has happened, and we would like to thank you all very much. We would like to get some pictures and maybe even some video which we will take with our cell phones as agreed with Commander Davis. Do any of you object to our using your names, etc.?"

Chloe took a quick look around at the team, and no one seemed to object. "I don't think it is necessary to paint us as heroes. We are just some people who care about our Orcas and marine wildlife and wish to keep it as healthy as possible."

"That is a perfect answer, Dr. Archer, and we will respect that request," Dave said, and Virginia nodded her assent as well.

Two days later, Mother backed slowly away from the beach and was greeted as she slowly swam out to rejoin her pod.

The TV Camera was focused on Virginia Grant

And that, ladies and gentlemen is a wrap. You have seen how a team of coordinated, well-meaning individuals can come to the aid of our animal friends and rescue a dying Orca pod Mother.

Please, take special care to dispose of your trash on shore in an appropriate container when you are near or on the water in our beautiful environment to protect the animals that share our world with us.

I AM VIRGINIA GRANT of CHANNEL 5 NEWS

Characters

The main characters in the story:

Jill: She is involved in the rescue and treatment of the Orca. She seems to be knowledgeable and resourceful, providing equipment like dive tanks and cushions to assist in the treatment of the Orca.

Jack: He is also involved in the rescue and treatment of the Orca. He is observant and provides useful insights, such as identifying the type of boat involved in the incident with the Orca.

Chloe: She is a veterinarian from the Oregon Institute of Marine Studies and is the specialist in charge of treating the Orca. She had previously worked on an injured young Orca two years ago.

Sam: He assists Jill and Chloe by fetching equipment like dive tanks and cushions. He also witnesses the incident with the Orca and provides a description of the boat involved.

Shirley: She is a game warden and a State Official who intervenes when a family is seen harming an Orca. She also seems to be involved in the rescue and treatment of the Orca.

Bobby: He is Chloe's husband and assists by fetching items like barbecue tongs from the boat.

Captain Miller: He is involved in the discussion about the incident with the Orca and provides insights about the challenges of identifying the boat involved.

Adrian: He provides medical advice about treating the Orca's injuries.

Biography

Charles P. Howerton, a retired Computer Science Professor from the Metropolitan State College of Denver, has always been a man of two worlds: the structured realm of computer science and the wild, untamed expanse of the ocean.

Born and raised in the heartland of America, Charles' fascination with the sea seemed unlikely. Yet, from a young age, he was captivated by the ocean's mysteries and its inhabitants, particularly the majestic Orca or killer whale. This fascination would become a lifelong passion, leading him on a journey spanned continents and decades.

In his professional life, Charles was a respected academic known for his innovative approach to computer science education. His tenure at the Metropolitan State College of Denver was marked by a dedication to his students and a commitment to advancing the field of computer science.

However, it was his passion for oceanic wildlife that truly defined him. Despite his inland roots, Charles became a staunch advocate for marine conservation. His love for the sea and its creatures was not just a hobby but a calling.

The recent events involving Orcas in Australia, Spain, and Portugal deeply moved Charles. Seeing these magnificent creatures playing with boats, yet facing numerous threats from human activities, inspired him to use his pen to raise awareness.

"Orca Tales" is the culmination of Charles' dual passions. It combines his analytical mind with his love for the ocean, weaving together a narrative that is as compelling as it is important. Charles hopes to inspire a new generation of conservationists through this book, just as the sea once inspired a young boy from the heartland.

Today, Charles P. Howerton is not just a retired professor; he is a voice for the voiceless, a champion for marine conservation, and a testament to the power of passion in driving change.